MANICURES and MURDER

A Texas-sized Murder Mystery Book 3

BY KERI LYNN

Published by Scrivenings Press LLC
15 Lucky Lane
Morrilton, Arkansas 72110
https://ScriveningsPress.com

Printed in the United States of America

Paperback ISBN 978-1-64917-339-3

eBook ISBN 978-1-64917-340-9

Editors: Erin R. Howard and Heidi Glick

Cover by Linda Fulkerson www.bookmarketinggraphics.com

All scriptures are taken from the KING JAMES VERSION (KJV): KING JAMES VERSION, public domain.

All characters are fictional, and any resemblance to real people, either factual or historical, is purely coincidental.

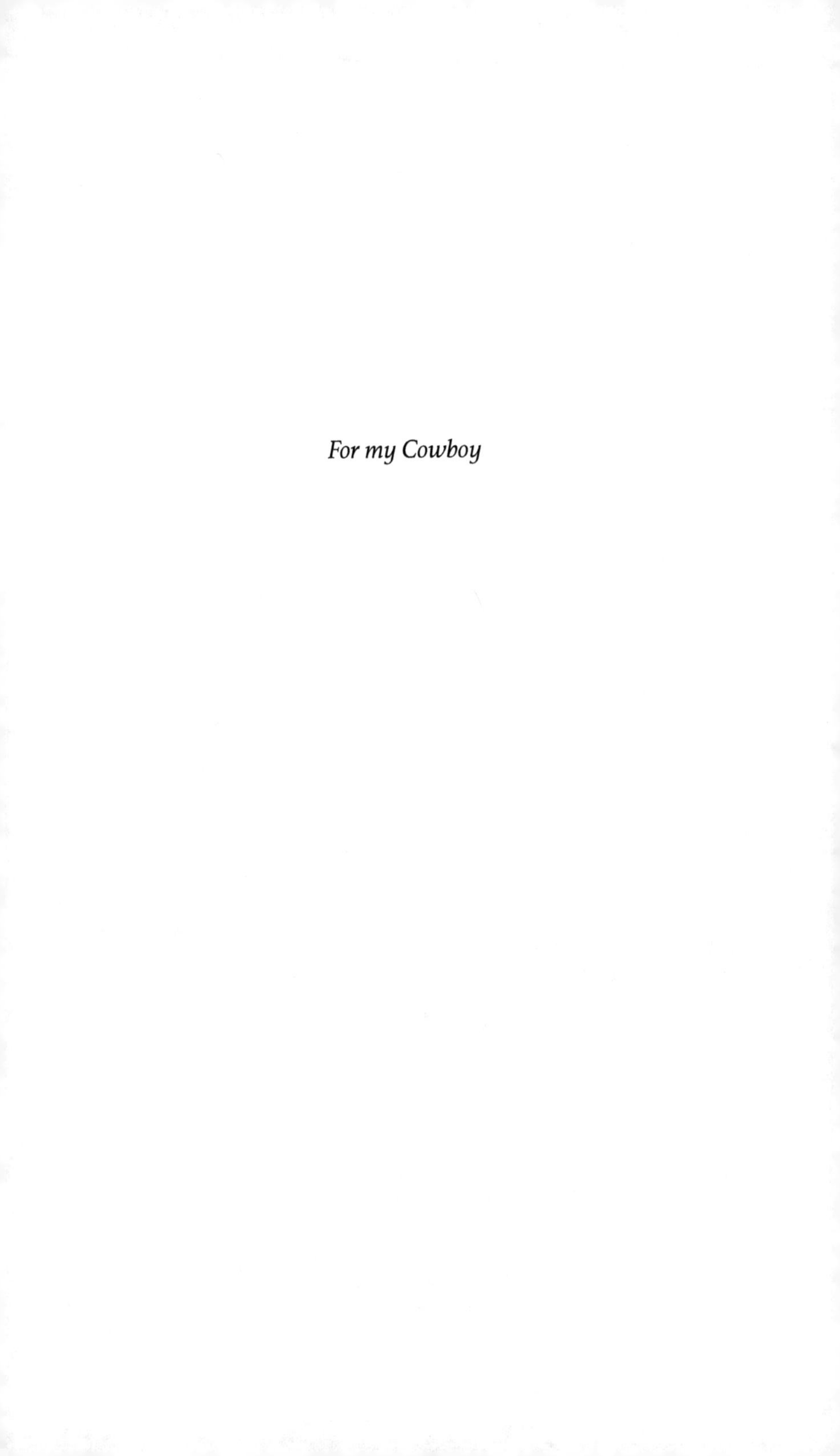

For my Cowboy

"Sarah! Someone help us!" Voice shrill, I fell to my knees next to my friend and fellow cosmetologist, Sarah Greene. One hand went to her throat to feel for a pulse while the other shook her shoulder in the dim morning light. "Sarah, can you hear me? Please, God, don't let this be happening."

Unable to find a pulse, I pushed Sarah's hair away from her face, revealing the gunshot wound in the middle of her forehead. The scream that left my lips echoed off the salon walls. Scrambling to my feet, I ran to the front door.

Shoving the door open, I stumbled across the wooden boardwalk and onto the street, still screaming. Across the road, business owners opened their doors and ran toward me, some pulling out their phones as they did so.

Tripping, I fell. Aubrey, owner of Flamingo Springs' bakery and diner, caught me before I hit the dirt.

"Lacey, what's wrong?" She pushed me upright, and I collapsed against her, trembling uncontrollably.

"Sarah's dead," I sobbed into her shoulder. "Oh, Aubrey, she's been shot in the head!"

A gasp of shock went through the surrounding crowd, and

Aubrey wrapped her arms around me even as Jeni, owner of the local jewelry store, took off at a run for my salon.

"Someone get Jeff!" Aubrey yelled. Running past us, Blaze barked orders into his phone.

"God help us," Marie, half owner of Esposito's, murmured behind me. Her husband, Vincent, echoed her as he made the sign of the cross.

The following minutes were a blur as Aubrey sat me down on the wooden sidewalk in front of her diner and rested a cold water bottle on the back of my neck as I pressed my face into my knees. Sweat pooled at the waistband of my jeans even as condensation from the bottle dripped down my neck and dampened my shirt collar.

Squeezing my eyes shut, I forced myself to take deep breaths, following Aubrey's instruction as she rubbed my back. I recalled how Sarah had looked, her brilliant blue eyes staring sightlessly at the salon ceiling. A bitter taste filled my mouth the same moment a wave of nausea slammed into me, and leaning forward, I threw up.

The crowd around me made sympathetic noises, their comforting words a dull roar in my ringing ears as I sobbed.

"Jeff's here," someone said.

I wiped my mouth as Flamingo Springs' doctor ran into my salon, the Christmas wreath on the door tilting as it shut behind him.

"It's no good," I whispered. "She's gone."

Sitting down next to me, Aubrey wrapped an arm around my shoulder after kicking dirt over my vomit. "Do you want to talk about it? It'd help oil your gears since Blaze is going to need to talk to you as soon as he can."

"She's gone," I repeated, the strong scent of cinnamon reaching my nose as Aubrey shifted positions. "I came into the salon at my usual time and found Sarah on the floor. I thought she was still in bed—I didn't hear her get up this morning, and I certainly didn't hear a gunshot."

"I don't think anyone did. Or else they would have called Blaze."

My salon's front door opened, and Jeni stepped out. Pausing in the doorway, she said something over her shoulder before pulling the door shut and crossing the street. Standing in front of me, her eyes were sad, mouth drawn into a thin line. "I'm so sorry, Lacey."

Shakily getting to my feet, I hugged my friend. Her sequined blouse scratched against my cheek. Her strong arms held me tight for a long moment, letting me cry into her shoulder as the shock wore off.

"Let's get her inside until Blaze is ready to talk," Aubrey told Jeni. "And if someone can get Pastor Brent down here, his presence is needed right now."

Keeping one arm wrapped around my shoulder, Jeni guided me down the sidewalk and through the front door of Aubrey's bakery. The usually welcome smells of breakfast foods and bakery delicacies were sickly sweet to my nose, and my stomach cramped.

Jerking away from Jeni, I bolted past the few patrons who'd remained inside and watched me with pity-filled stares. Once I made my way into the snowman-decorated restroom, I collapsed, dry heaving into the toilet. Biting my tongue, the metallic taste of blood filled my mouth as my tears dripped to the floor. Jeni crouched next to me, one hand splayed across my back, the other holding tissues to my mouth to catch the blood I was too nauseated to swallow.

"God help her," she whispered. A male voice rang out in the dining area, interrupting the rest of her prayer. "We're in here," she called.

Pastor Brent entered the small restroom a moment later, his

wife, Suzanne, standing in the doorway, one hand covering her mouth.

Patting my shoulder after handing me the blood-soaked tissue, Jeni went to join her, letting Brent kneel next to me on the cold tiles. The scent of lemons and bleach surrounded us.

Resting a warm hand on my head, he began to pray, his voice strong, and the nausea left me not long after.

"Lacey! Where is she?" The familiar voice of my ex-boyfriend, Cody Jackson, cut Brent off. The sweet scent of hay, leather, and musky aftershave reached my nose just as Cody shoved past Jeni and into the crowded restroom.

"Cody, I told you to wait," Aubrey snapped at him from the hallway, but he ignored her, pushing Brent out of the way to take me into his arms.

"Blaze called me," he said, holding me tight against his chest, and I buried my face in his shoulder. Though we'd broken things off for good the previous month, I needed him, and he knew it.

"I'm glad you came," I whispered, my tears soaking his plaid shirt. "Cody, I don't know what to do."

"You don't have to." He cupped the back of my head. "I'm here, and I'll take care of you."

"She needs to get upstairs." Aubrey's voice was firm as she still stood in the hallway behind Suzanne and Jeni.

"I don't want to be alone." I pulled away from Cody, looking at my friends over his shoulder. Quick to speak, Suzanne leaned around Brent to do so as her husband went to stand in the doorway. "Oh, honey, we won't leave you alone, I promise. Cody, can you help her upstairs?"

The professional bull rider and ranch owner looked down at me, blue eyes narrowed. "Can you stand?"

When I shook my head, the room spun, he let me go and stood. Crouching a bit, he slid an arm under my knees, the other wrapping around my back, picking me up as he stood.

Boots loud on the white floor, he turned, careful not to hit the counter with my feet, everyone moving out of the way and letting us enter the hallway.

"Aubrey," Brey called from the kitchen. "I hate to interrupt, but I'm getting overwhelmed in here."

"Be right there," Aubrey yelled back. Digging in her pocket, she pulled out a set of keys and handed them to Brent. "Go ahead and unlock my apartment. Feel free to use anything she might need."

"Will do." Brent took the keys and headed into the kitchen toward the back door. "Kinda wish Misty was here, if I'm being honest."

"You and me both," Aubrey sighed, going to stand in front of the industrial-sized griddle in the kitchen. Brey handed her a stack of orders before scurrying past us and back into the dining room with a coffee carafe.

The sudden change in scenery as Cody carried me through the kitchen and out the back door had my head spinning again, and I rested it against his chest. Shivers shook my body despite the warm air that surrounded us as he stepped out onto the back porch. The sky above seemed painfully bright, and the sudden tightening in my lungs had me twisting away from him and almost falling to the ground.

"Lacey," he grunted, struggling to hold on to me as my quick movements caused him to drop to one knee.

"I can't breathe," I gasped, jerking away from him and falling on the wooden planks. Splinters stabbed my hands as I opened my mouth, trying to gulp in air, and black pinpricks began to swim across my vision. "Cody, I can't breathe!"

Legs tangled together, Cody rested one hand on my back, the other going to my chest, just under my collarbone, his touch warm against my cold skin. "Through the nose, out through the mouth."

Brent, Suzanne, and Jeni stood a few feet away, giving me space. Jeni wiped her eyes, lips moving as she quietly prayed.

"Come on, Lacey girl," Cody urged me. "Breathe through your nose. Yeah, like that. Hold it for a second, if you can. Atta girl." Rubbing my back, he shifted until he could wrap his arm around me, his lips almost touching my ear as he spoke.

The sharp jabs of pain that filled my lungs subsided as I focused on breathing. Shoving my hair behind my ears, I scrubbed my hands down my thighs, the feeling of denim rough against my palms.

"That's it." Cody squeezed me against him, the scruff on his chin rough against my ear. "Just keep doing exactly that." Pausing, he smoothed a hand down my hair. "Do you want me to carry you, or do you want to try to walk?"

Pulling away, I stared into his worried eyes before shaking my head as my pulse began to slow. Hands braced on the wooden porch, I pushed myself to my feet, Cody keeping a hand on my arm as he stood with me.

"I think I can walk," I said. My first step was wobbly, and I grimaced, Cody's arm looped around my waist as my stomach clenched. "At least, I'm going to try to."

"Take your time, Lacey girl," Cody said softly, guiding me toward the stairs. Brent stood at the top, working to unlock the door, muttering something about Aubrey needing to oil the mechanisms.

Placing my foot on the first step, I took a deep breath, then another, before grabbing the guardrail and easing onto the second step. Falling in behind me, Cody kept one hand on my back, Jeni behind him while Suzanne stayed on the porch and talked quietly into her phone.

Once I reached the landing, legs shaking, Brent held the door open, one hand extended to me. Grasping it, I let him lead me into Aubrey's small living room.

"Sit here," he said, nudging me toward the couch. Once I'd

settled onto the worn cushions, he crossed over into Aubrey's pristine kitchen and ran a glass of water and pressed it into my clammy hands.

Cody's phone rang as he sat next to me, Brent taking the rocking chair across the room. Jeni busied herself in the kitchen, filling the coffee pot and digging out the can of grounds from the cabinet.

"This is Cody," my ex-boyfriend said, voice rough. Glancing at me, he nodded, eyes narrowing as he ran a hand through his hair. "Yeah, Pastor Brent is here. So is Jeni. No, she's lucid. All right. We'll be waiting." Hitting a button on his phone, he slipped it into his pocket. "That was Blaze. He'll be up in a few minutes. They've about got the scene secured, and he wants to interview you right away."

Pulling my legs up so my heels rested on the cushion's edge, I wrapped my arms around my knees. "I'll do my best, but there's not much to tell him." Staring at the small, brightly lit pine tree in the corner, my eyes burned as I focused on the multi-colored lights.

"That's okay," Brent assured me. "Just answer his questions the best you can." Shifting in the rocker, he crossed one leg over the other before continuing. "I know this seems like we're rushing you, but is there anyone we should call for you? We can't call anyone on Sarah's behalf until Blaze gives the all clear, but perhaps your mother? For support?"

"Oh, my!" Straightening, I turned to Cody, grabbing his arm. "Dalton. Cody, you have to tell Dalton."

Muscles tensing beneath my hands, Cody met my gaze as the smell of percolating coffee filled the air. "He's going to be devastated. I don't even know how to tell him."

"Dalton?" Brent asked, accepting the slice of banana bread Jeni handed him on a saucer. Green eyes bright, I knew she was making notes of everything being said as she set a glass of water on the coffee table next to me. "Is he that new ranch hand you just hired?"

Cody nodded. "Yes. He moved here to try to patch things up with Sarah."

"They were on the right track too." I closed my eyes for a moment. "She told me only a few days ago they were thinking about getting married."

Cody stood. "I'll be out on the landing. It'll be best to call my foreman first so he can be with Dalton when I break the news."

Closing the door behind him, Cody's voice faded out, and letting out a sigh, Jeni sat next to me, wiping her hands on her legs as she shook her head. "Lord have mercy on us," she said. Brent echoed her as he drummed his fingers on the armrest of his chair. "This world has lost its mind, and it's the innocent who suffer the most."

Pulling one leg up beneath herself, Jeni took a sip of water from the glass she'd filled in the kitchen, forehead wrinkled as she frowned. Settling back onto the couch, I glanced around us as Cody's voice rumbled outside the door.

Aubrey's apartment was nothing special, but I always felt at home when I visited her. Staring at the various pictures she'd staggered across the walls—garland strung between them—the tension in my shoulders slowly drained away.

"We had such big plans, you know." I rested the glass on my knee. Jeni and Brent looked at me, both quiet, waiting for me to go on, and after a moment, I did. "With two of us running the salon, we could offer twice the service, and we were planning a girls' trip to the Bahamas for Valentine's Day."

Looking down, I cleared my throat, eyes stinging as tears began to fill them again. "She was one of my best friends in beauty school, and it was so incredible to get back in touch after drifting apart over the years. Having a business partner who was also a friend ..." Trailing off, I stared blankly at the wall above the door. "And now she's gone."

"Oh, Lacey." Setting her plate down, Jeni wrapped an arm around my shoulder as tears slipped down my cheeks, my swollen eyes stinging as my throat tightened.

"God, we need you," Brent whispered from his chair.

The sound of Cody reopening the door interrupted the soft prayer, and looking over my shoulder, I watched as Blaze followed him in. Green eyes crinkled at the corners, his mouth was a thin line, and the sigh he let out was heavy.

"Let's sit at the table." Blaze gestured toward the small dinette in the middle of Aubrey's kitchen. Glancing around the full apartment, he frowned. "Only one of you gets to stay, so decide who that should be."

"I'll stay," Cody said, cutting off Jeni, who pulled out a chair for me, but I shook my head.

"I want Pastor Brent to stay." Sitting on the wooden chair that had seen better days, I propped my elbows on the table, crossing my ankles.

Brent took the spot next to me as Blaze sat across from us, opening his laptop after looking at his phone. Cody and Jeni quietly let themselves out.

"There was no sign of forced entry, so Sarah must have known who killed her." Blaze's voice grew quiet as he stared at his computer screen. "With no security cameras outside, there's not much for me to go on, but at least I know this wasn't a random murder."

"So what now?" Brent asked quietly.

"Now," Blaze answered, "we start here. Get all the info possible and chase leads." Glancing at me, he cleared his throat. "Ready?" he asked, the tan of his shirt bringing out the brown flecks in his eyes.

"No. But I don't have a choice."

"Yeah," Blaze murmured. "And I'm sorry." Looking down at

his computer, he tapped a few keys. "Let's start with how you knew the victim."

A sad smile twisted my lips, and Brent reached out, patting my arm as another tear fell to the table.

"Sarah and I met in beauty school and became roommates. We lost touch over the years, and after I moved here, I never heard from her again. Life was so busy for both of us, so I was surprised when she reached out a few weeks ago and asked to visit me."

"Any reason for that visit beyond just wanting to catch up?" Blaze typed away, ignoring the phone buzzing on his belt.

"Healing from a broken relationship. But other than that, nothing I'm aware of. It was so good to see her again, and we hit it off so well I asked her to join my business here, as she'd left her position in Miami."

"Any mention of an abusive ex, or any hint she was in danger, or was ever involved in something that could bring her harm?"

Blaze looked at me as he asked, sucking on his teeth while he waited for my answer. The faint line of a mustache darkened the skin above his mouth, making him look older than he was.

Shaking my head, I clasped my hands in front of me, licking suddenly dry lips. "No. She never mentioned anything like that. Dalton was her ex, and he came here. They repaired their relationship and were talking about marriage."

"What about her former job? Anything there? Did she leave for a reason?"

Frowning, I met Blaze's gaze. "Actually, that's the one thing she wouldn't talk about. Sarah is—*was*, such an open person about everything, but she wouldn't talk about it beyond saying she and the salon owner didn't see eye to eye on a lot of things and she left on very bad terms and almost lost her license."

"I see." Scratching the side of his nose, Blaze typed

something out before clicking the keypad mouse. "I'll see if I can find out which salon and try to talk to the owner."

Shifting, he took a sip of water from a cup Jeni had placed in front of him before leaving. "Let's talk about last night and this morning. Did she act unusual the last time you saw her?"

"Honestly," I sighed, burying my face in my hands, "I don't know. It was like getting to know her all over again, so I wasn't too familiar with all her moods and quirks yet." Looking back up, I frowned. "I'm sorry."

Blaze nodded. "And what about early this morning? Jeff estimated her time of death to be about 3:00 a.m. Were you up at all during that time?"

"No. I went to bed at 11:00 p.m. and didn't wake up until my alarm went off at 6:30 a.m. I thought she was still asleep in her room and didn't know anything was wrong until ..." Voice trailing off, I looked toward Brent, who gave me an encouraging nod. "Until I walked into my salon and saw her on the floor. From there on, it's a little blurry. I just remember running outside."

"Well," Blaze said, closing his laptop, "it's not much to go on, but the part about her leaving her job on bad terms interests me." Standing, he slid the computer into a leather bag before draining his glass of water. "Lacey, at this point, you're not a suspect, but you are a person of interest, which is standard. I'd ask you not to leave town, and if you think of anything that might be helpful, you have my number."

Walking past me, he paused, dropping his hand to my shoulder. Giving it a gentle squeeze, he waited until I looked at him to speak. "Might be best if you stay somewhere else for a while. Aubrey would love to have you stay with her, and so would Jeni. When you're ready to go pack a bag, just let me or Terri know, and we'll meet you there."

Letting his hand drop away, he strode toward the door,

boots loud on the wood floor, and twisting in my chair, I called after him. "Promise me you'll find who did this, Blaze."

Turning, he gave me a long look. "No promises on that, but I do promise to do everything I possibly can. Deal?"

Biting my lip, I nodded, and once he'd left, I turned to Brent.

"Whoever did this can't get away," I whispered. "I won't let that happen. I don't care what I have to do, or where I have to go. I'm going to find them."

2

____

"Sarah would've hated this." Dalton Hennings' shoulder brushed mine as he gestured around the room, his voice grew raspy from unshed tears.

Nodding, I clenched my hands in my lap as we sat in the corner of Aubrey's diner. It'd been two days since Sarah's murder, and Brent had asked to have a small memorial service for the cosmetologist after learning she had no contact with her family.

"Tell me about it." I shifted in my chair.

Aubrey moved around the cheerfully decorated dining room she'd rearranged so everyone could mingle. The silver tinsel she'd hung from the ceiling moved as the vent on the wall blew out warm air, and Christmas carols drifted from the radio on the counter. One hand holding a pitcher of lemonade, she offered napkins to those eating the free cupcakes displayed on the counter, her smile wide as she gave someone a hug.

"Sarah hated any form of attention, and this would have driven her crazy," Dalton said.

Sipping my glass of water, I glanced at the cowboy next to me before setting it back on the table.

His curly black hair needed a trim, and stubble covered his normally smooth jaw. Green eyes bloodshot, the thirty-something year old cowhand's shoulders slumped forward, and his jeans sported a tear at the knee.

"I know it's such a useless thing to say, but if you need anything ..." Voice trailing off, I waited until Sarah's fiancé looked at me before finishing my thought. "I didn't know her like you did, but she was a good friend, and I was glad to have her in my life."

Eyes meeting mine, Dalton cleared his throat. "I won't need anything, but thank you for the offer. That means a lot." Hands clasped between his knees, he let out a deep sigh. "We were planning on having kids, you know. Maybe buying some land from Cody and having a small spot to call ours while I worked my way up at his ranch. Mason was gonna help me crunch all the numbers to see how soon we could manage it."

"She mentioned that." Taking another sip of my water, I blinked back tears as I gave Mason, Dalton's friend and Cody's third in command, a weak smile as he took a seat across the room. "It's not fair."

Dalton snorted. "Life never is. And when I track down who did it, they'll find out real fast how unfair life can really be."

Glancing at him, I licked my lips. "I know Blaze already interviewed you, but any idea who might be behind it? With no trail, he said it's starting to look like a senseless murder, but nothing premeditated."

"Oh, it was planned out. Have no doubt about that." Voice low, Dalton clenched his jaw. "She left that salon in Florida on bad terms, Lacey. Someone there had something to do with it, mark my words."

"But why?" I pressed, leaning closer to him, our voices low, not willing to catch anyone's attention. I had no need to worry though, as no one seemed to pay us any mind.

"Miami is many things. Absolutely bogged down with drugs

is one of them. One of Sarah's coworkers was messed up on drugs, and I think that's why she was murdered. She knew too much."

"Did you tell Blaze all this?" My eyes followed the sheriff in question as he checked his phone.

"Yes." Dalton sat back in his chair. "And he said he was looking into it, but so far, there's no proof anyone in the salon was involved with drugs."

Getting to his feet, Dalton looked down at me. "If something happens to me, promise me you'll keep searching until you find Sarah's killer."

Standing, I stared up at the tall cowboy. "You're scaring me. Nothing is going to happen to you."

Dalton leaned so close I could smell the coffee on his breath, his voice serious. "It wasn't a random murder, and you know it. If they went after her, they'll come after me, and then they'll come after you until everyone she knew is dead."

Stepping back, he lifted his chin. "Stay close to Cody. He'll keep you safe. But promise me. Promise me you won't let it go."

"I promise," I whispered, and after a moment of fierce eye contact, Dalton nodded before moving past me toward the door.

Chills ran down my spine as he disappeared into the night, and the fear I'd never see him again settled into my stomach.

Dalton wasn't wrong when he'd said Sarah had been murdered for knowing something. From the first day of moving in with me, she was hesitant to talk about her past job and refused to discuss anything but the future. Having deleted all her social media accounts and switched bank accounts immediately upon moving to Flamingo Springs, it had seemed like she was starting over, but now I wondered if my beauty school friend had been trying to disappear.

"You okay?" Sitting down next to me, Aubrey offered me a

small smile along with a pat on the knee, the diamond on her ring finger catching in the light.

Sighing, I met my friend's blue eyes. "I don't think this is as simple as it looks, Aubrey."

Frowning, the bakery owner leaned back in her chair, its metal hinges squeaking as she did so, the low murmur of those around us covering up our conversation. "What do you mean?"

"Dalton just told me he thinks he's next." Voice low, I bit my lip. "I'm really glad I'm staying with you right now and neither one of us is alone."

Glancing across the room to where her fiancé showed Jesse something on his phone, Aubrey's mouth thinned. "Did Dalton speak to Blaze about it?"

"He did. And Blaze is doing everything he can, but Dalton was pretty sure he's next."

"Hopefully, he doesn't try to borrow trouble." Getting to her feet, Aubrey gave me a concerned look. "But I'll mention it to Blaze, just in case he's right."

Thanking her, I slouched in my chair, staring at the floor in front of me. Dalton's words rang in my ears, and I couldn't forget the sincerity with which he'd spoken them.

Not much of a religious woman, my thoughts turned to God, and I sent up a small prayer, the very act feeling foreign. I hoped I wasn't the only one praying, because it seemed like things were about to get much worse.

"Lacey?"

Aubrey's whisper interrupted my restless sleep, which was full of flashbacks from the last few days. Sitting up on the couch in her living room, I blinked at her in the dim light of the Christmas tree as she crouched over me. One hand holding her phone to her chest, she pressed the other against the front of her thigh.

"Is everything okay?" Words slightly slurred, I struggled to blink, trying to bring her into focus as I pulled my legs to my chest, the blanket scrunched up around me.

Sitting down next to me, Aubrey rubbed the back of her neck. The pink satin pajama set she wore shimmered in the colored light, and after a moment, she looked at me.

"Dalton's dead, Lacey. They found his body about forty minutes ago just outside Cody's ranch."

All feelings of grogginess left, and I was suddenly cold. Hands covering my mouth, I stared at my friend. "Aubrey. No."

She nodded. "Cody and Mason found Dalton after he sent them a blank text. He was in his truck, two tires blown out. Whoever it was killed him with a single shot to the head, just like with Sarah. Blaze isn't sure yet, but it's probably the same gun used to kill Sarah."

Placing my feet on the floor, I resisted the urge to vomit. "He was right. And he told me I'd be next." Looking at Aubrey, I could hear the panic in my voice. "Aubrey, we're not safe."

"We're as safe as we can be right now," she told me, shifting positions, a lemon scent teasing my nose as she did so. "Blaze already figured you might be a target, and this is the safest place until he gets back." Pausing, she checked her phone, reading something before continuing. "That's the problem with a small town—the police department is also small."

"Two lives gone, just like that," I said, pressing my hands to my face, eyes burning with tears as I remembered the pain in Dalton's eyes. "Two people with dreams and hopes just gone."

"My question is, why was Dalton outside Cody's ranch at three in the morning?" Wrapping an arm around my shoulder, Aubrey's voice was strained. "That means he left once everyone had gone to bed and was on his way back. What did he find between when the ranch hands went to bed and 3:00 a.m.?"

Hands shaking, I placed them in my lap, leaning against Aubrey. "More than that, who found him?"

Stifling a yawn, Aubrey leaned back against the cushions,

pulling her arm away as I curled up against the side of the couch. "You're sure Sarah never said anything that might point Blaze in the right direction?"

Shaking my head, I wiped my hand over my eyes. "No. All she told me was things ended badly at her old salon and she needed to start over. Dalton followed her here to fix their relationship."

"Dalton told Blaze he suspected drugs are involved," Aubrey said, tapping her phone against her leg. "But this seems extreme."

"Ryan was killed by his own brother all because of drugs," I reminded her, and we fell silent as I thought about the young store owner's death and the arrest of the mastermind behind it, local favorite, Seth. Though in the end, Seth admitted his crimes and surrendered his life to God, Ryan was still gone, and a gunshot wound had left Deputy Stetson partially paralyzed.

"People will do anything," I whispered. "No matter the price, no matter who it hurts." Picking up my phone and unplugging it from its charging cord, I tapped Cody's name in my contact list. Listening to it ring, I looked over at Aubrey. "Maybe Cody can give us a few more details."

The rest of my words were cut of when my ex-boyfriend answered his phone.

"Lacey?" His voice sounded strained.

"Are you okay?" Hands shaking, I pressed my phone against my ear, wishing I could be with Cody. Even though we'd parted ways on bad terms, I still cared for the rodeo star and hated the thought of him facing this alone.

"About as okay as you are. Lacey, whatever is going on is bad, really bad. Blaze and a few boys from a county over have been tracing Dalton's tracks, and they can see where someone chased him for about five miles. His truck is full of bullet holes, and he was so close to the ranch before they got him. So close."

Choking up, Cody fell silent, and for the second time that

night, I sent up a feeble prayer as Mason said something, his words muffled.

"I wish I was there." As soon as the words left my mouth, I regretted them. Though Aubrey remained silent, the look she gave me was more than a little surprised. The bakery owner had been witness to the disaster of a relationship I'd had with Cody for the last three years and had consoled me more than once as I'd cried over the rodeo star.

"That means a lot," Cody told me, and in the background, I could hear the low murmur of male voices and the distinct sound of a dispatch radio. "But I'm okay."

The rest of his words were cut off when Blaze said something, and after a moment, Cody ended the call.

Looking at Aubrey, I set my phone down. "What now?"

Staring back at me, my friend's blue eyes were narrowed. "What do you mean?"

"What do we do now?"

Leaning forward, Aubrey picked up a piece of lint from the floor, turning it over between her fingers for a moment before answering. She finally spoke, a measure of anger in her voice. "Looks to me like we've got two options. Either we can sit back and pray and hope for the best while Blaze does what he can, or ..." Looking back at me, she clenched her jaw. "We can still pray and also do everything we can to find out who's behind this and ensure they pay for what they've done."

Holding up a hand, she cut me off before I could even get one word out. "When Mabel attacked others after she murdered Vicki, I had a moment where I had to decide between letting fear control me and hiding, or getting involved and doing what I could to stop her before she hurt someone else."

Unable to meet Aubrey's harsh stare any longer, I glanced down at my hands, which were clenched together so tightly my knuckles were white.

"I didn't use to be so timid," I whispered. "As a teen, I was a barrel racer and the only girl in my county to join steer wrestling. Then, in my early twenties, I was a bull rider, and I almost always won. I wasn't afraid of anything, or anyone, for that matter. Sometimes, when I see you, Aubrey, I see who I used to be. Strong, confident, and able to push forward even when afraid."

"What changed?" Aubrey's voice grew soft as she drew her legs up on the couch, all traces of sleepiness gone from her tone.

"Daddy died." Sniffling, I scrubbed a hand across my eyes. "The one person who always had my back, who always cheered me on and told me I could do anything with God by my side, was gone, and I didn't even get to say goodbye."

"You're afraid to get attached to anything because there's a chance you could lose it."

The compassion that filled my friend's voice surprised me, and when I looked at her, she shrugged.

"I've been there. Coming here, opening the diner, that was easy compared to choosing to let Blaze into my heart." Pausing, she reached out and rested a warm hand on my knee as it bounced up and down. "And letting God into my heart? Easily the scariest thing I've ever done."

"So what got you to that point where you decided to just do it afraid?"

Sighing, Aubrey patted my knee before pulling her hand away. "Misty, actually. One night when she helped me repaint the kitchen, she asked me two hard questions. Had I decided I was incapable of doing something because of fear? And had I created an idea of God based on the bias of others instead of seeking Him myself?"

Tilting her head, Aubrey gave me a small smile. "Maybe, she said, I should try letting someone into my heart and see if they're supposed to be there or not instead of never unlocking the door and never letting them in. So, we can sit and feel helpless and afraid, or, we can get busy, still feel afraid, but actually be doing something."

I stared at my friend for a long moment, her wise words taking me by surprise. Biting my lip, I stood, the blanket falling to the floor.

"Let's make some coffee. We have a suspect list to start."

TWO HOURS LATER, I drained the last of my fourth cup of coffee. Setting the empty mug down, I stared at the list Aubrey and I had compiled on the back of her electric bill. The straight, clean lines of her handwriting stood out next to the loopy letters I'd written. The top half of the paper was filled with names, while the bottom was crammed with notes and partial thoughts, as well as a few doodles here and there.

Tapping her pen against her teeth, Aubrey squinted in the pale glow of the overhead kitchen light before picking up a slice of toast.

"Obviously, Sarah's former boss and coworkers are the main suspects, but since Blaze is already pursuing that lead, I think we should focus on who is after that."

"It's terrible to even think of Dalton being the one who murdered Sarah, but I agree."

Running my tongue over my teeth, I took a deep breath, the smell of coffee and cranberry bagels filling my nose. Looking at the list, I studied the star Aubrey had drawn next to Dalton's name before looking back up at my friend.

"Where do we start?" Aubrey glanced at me, eyes slightly bloodshot, as she bit into a piece of toast.

"We could start with her belongings." I slouched in my chair, toying with my pen. "But I bet Blaze took everything."

"And he probably seized all of Dalton's stuff too," Aubrey mused, speaking around the toast.

"So Cody's ranch is our best bet. Obviously, I'm new at this, but maybe we'll find something he didn't."

"Not necessarily. But rather, Cody's ranch hands will be more likely to talk to us than Blaze. Some have things they'd prefer to keep hidden, and if they get involved with Blaze, he'll find out. They don't have to worry about that with two meddling women."

"Will Blaze be mad we're doing this?" Leaning forward, I poured myself another cup of coffee from the carafe Aubrey had left on the table, steam rising into the air.

Aubrey scratched her neck. Her black hair shone in the early morning sun that peeked around the kitchen curtain.

"Honestly? Yes. But he already knows we're gonna get involved, so as long as we don't get in his way or do anything dangerous, he'll let us be."

"And if we find something?" Setting the carafe down, I picked up a bagel.

"Depends on what it is," Aubrey replied. "But let's worry about getting to Cody's ranch first." Pointing at me with the piece of toast she still held, her brow lowered. "And more than that, how you're gonna feel being around Cody so much. The man obviously still loves you, so you need to be prepared for that."

Shrugging, I fiddled with my bagel. "Well, I don't feel the same, so it won't be a problem."

Aubrey pinned me with a stern yet compassionate look. "I'll leave that one alone," she said after a moment.

My stomach fluttered. Maybe I could change the subject. "Will you be able to take time away from the bakery?"

"Terri's off the next four days from the force, and I'm certain she'd love to pick up the hours. So it won't be a problem."

"If only Misty was here," I sighed, setting my bagel back down, losing my appetite. "She's good at this stuff. I'm not."

"You did great when we were trying to catch Royce," Aubrey said, and we were silent for a moment, remembering the events following the murder of his brother Ryan.

Slapping the table, Aubrey stood. "Well, we're not gonna get anything done by sitting around drinking coffee and pining over the fact Misty's on her honeymoon and not here helping us. I'm assuming Cody's ranch is wide awake, so let's get dressed and head there before Blaze thinks to stop us."

Sensing my hesitation, she leaned down and wrapped her arms around me. "We're gonna find who did this, Lacey. I promise."

"That's what scares me," I whispered, a single tear falling onto the list in front of me, the ink slowly blurring beneath it, melting the letters together. "Because when we find them, I'm going to do everything I can to make them pay."

3

F lipping the sun visor down, Aubrey carefully steered her jeep onto the dirt road to Cody's ranch house. Heat set on low, the almost thirty-minute drive had been quiet, both of us lost in thought.

Dalton's bullet-riddled truck was still parked on the side of the road, the yellow caution tape surrounding it fluttering in the slight breeze. Staring down at my hands, I refused to look up until it was well behind us. A sad silence filled the vehicle.

"This isn't exactly the easiest decision to make," I finally said. "But I know it's the right one. Even though I'm more scared than I've ever been in my life, I'm gonna see this through."

"That's how I felt after Vicki was murdered," Aubrey said softly. "Knowing the right thing to do but being terrified to do it."

Braking, Aubrey brought the jeep to a halt in front of Cody's massive ranch home, dust swirling around the two Australian Shepherds that ran up to our doors barking. Luna and Henry were both three years old, and I'd missed them when Cody and I had parted ways.

Putting the vehicle in park, Aubrey glanced over at me as Cody appeared in the doorway of the barn that loomed to our left. His foreman, Greg, stood next to him.

"Sure you want to let him back in your life?" Aubrey asked.

"No." I took off my seatbelt off and eased my door open, careful not to hit the dogs, which were still barking at us. "And I never will be."

Sliding out of my seat, I slipped my phone into my back pocket before bending and petting Luna as she sat at my feet, her barks turning into pants. Tongue warm, she licked my hand, and I took a moment to crouch down and rub her ears, breathing in the heavy smells of dust and animals.

The sound of boots crunching on gravel alerted me to Cody's presence right before he rounded the front of the vehicle. White hat tilted back, he came to a stop a few feet away from me and hooked his thumbs in his belt loops.

Looking up at him, my stomach tightened as I remembered all the plans we'd once had to get married and have a few kids when he'd retired from the rodeo. All that had changed in the matter of a few minutes when he'd decided it was easier to walk away from me than face his commitment issues.

Glancing back at the dog, I rubbed her ears a moment longer before standing, the thin hoodie I wore feeling too tight around my neck.

"Cody."

I stared into his familiar blueberry-colored eyes. The sound of Aubrey slamming the car door shut was faint as Cody met my gaze.

"Lacey."

After a moment's hesitation, he stepped around Luna as she rolled over and gathered me into his arms. It was in me to push him away, but when his chest heaved against mine, I shoved the memories of our relationship aside. Looping my arms around his waist, I held him close as he buried his face in my neck, his tears hot against my skin.

Cody and Dalton had been childhood friends, and, like Sarah and me, had lost contact over the years. When Dalton had moved back to Texas to pursue Sarah, Cody had been overjoyed to have his friend around. Losing him only a few weeks later was clearly affecting him, and I found myself yet again praying to a God I still wasn't sure I believed in.

After a moment, Cody pulled away, keeping his arms around my waist.

"I'd say I'm glad to see you, but I know why you're here." Voice raspy, his look was stern.

"And why am I here?" Quirking an eyebrow, I took a step back, putting space between us, and he let his arms drop to his sides.

Glancing over his shoulder at Aubrey as she rounded the front of her vehicle, ending her phone call as she did so, he let out a short laugh.

"Lacey, if there's one thing I've learned, if Aubrey's around, you know trouble's brewing. Ain't no secret she solved the case with Mabel and that you and Misty figured out what was goin' on with Seth and Royce. You're here to see if Blaze missed anything."

Aubrey propped a hand on her hip and looked up at the tall rancher, squinting in the bright morning sun. The sound of cows lowing in the pasture behind the house was a pleasant backdrop to the chickens that clucked around our feet. "Got a problem with that?"

Tilting his hat down, Cody gave us a long look, chewing the inside of his lip, a habit he'd picked up after quitting chewing tobacco.

"No," he drawled. "I reckon I don't. Two people have been murdered in less than a week. The more people snooping around the better, I say, long as those who aren't trained to do so watch their steps and don't get themselves hurt."

"That's fair," Aubrey agreed, absentmindedly scratching the cattle dog that now sat on her feet and looked up at her.

"What's fair?" Greg appeared behind the ranch owner, holding his hat by his side. Straw-colored hair tousled, his green T-shirt sported a tear on the left arm and was speckled with mud and loose bits of hay.

Not giving anyone time to answer, he went on, "Ahh. Letting them think they'll find something so they feel better?"

"Cool it, Cowboy," Aubrey told him. "We're not here to start a fight. If there's anything we can do to help, we want to make sure we're doing it."

Brown eyes squinting, Greg made a show of leaning over and spitting out a mouthful of dip. "Just one more thing to have to worry about," he muttered. "And we've already got more than enough to take care of."

"Greg." Cody turned to his foreman. "I've given them the all clear. Pretty doubtful they'll find anything, but it can't hurt."

Greg's brow lowered as he stared at his boss of several years. When it became evident Cody wasn't budging in his decision, he looked away, slapping his hat against his thigh before plopping it back on his head.

"It's your call, boss." Digging his can of dip from his back pocket, Greg made a show of packing his lip before walking away. Mason said something to him when he reached the barn, making the foreman laugh as they disappeared inside.

"Don't mind Greg." Cody turned back to face us. "He'll come around. It's just a lot to take in right now, and everyone's already on edge with Blaze snooping around."

Looking over at me, he lifted an eyebrow. "I was gettin' ready to ride out to my south pasture and check something, if you'd like to ride along."

"Don't worry about me," Aubrey said cheerfully, still petting

Henry. "I'll find my own way around." The sarcasm in her voice wasn't lost on me but obviously was on Cody because his lips parted in a grin.

"Good!" Holding out his hand, Cody waited for me to take it before heading toward the barn, leaving Aubrey to roll her eyes at me.

"What is it you're checking out?" Hurrying to keep up with the tall bull rider, I almost tripped, and he shortened his stride.

"She speaks!" Cody teased, squeezing my hand like he'd done a million times before.

Shrugging, I kicked at a piece of gravel as we crossed the driveway, the sun warm on the back of my neck. I glanced over my shoulder, watching Aubrey head in the opposite direction toward the back of the house.

I shifted my gaze back to Cody. "Guess I just don't have a lot to say right now."

"That's not the Lacey Baker I know." Cody's leg brushed mine as we entered the barn. "You always have something to say." At the other end, Greg and Mason worked on a tractor, both laughing as music played.

"You don't know me anymore," I said softly, and Cody stopped, turning to face me, dropping my hand.

"Don't you think there's a better time to address that?" The muscles in his forearms tensed.

"I do. And I wasn't addressing it, but since you brought it up, we need to agree I'm not here for anything related to us. I'm here to find out who murdered my friend and your ranch hand. Deal?"

"Deal." Turning away, Cody headed to the stall where his horse, Garth, was saddled and patiently waiting for his rider. "Take your pick and saddle up."

"Now that we got that out of the way, what is it you want to look at?" I went to the opposite wall and picked up a saddle. The weight was both strange and familiar to me, as it'd been a long time since I'd done anything ranch or horse related, and the stretch across my back felt good.

"Might be nothing, and it probably is." Cody fiddled with Garth's reins, the yellow overhead lights casting his face in shadows beneath his hat. "So I haven't said anything to Blaze. Honeysuckle was on the floorboard in Dalton's truck, and it only grows in the south pasture by that shallow ravine where we lost that calf last year. We haven't used that pasture in two months and won't be doing so for another three. Doesn't make sense for him to have been out there."

"So you'd like to see if there's anything else there." Walking a few stalls down from him, I set the saddle down before opening the wooden gate. Brooks, the mare behind it, nickered when she recognized me.

"It's probably nothing." Despite his efforts, Cody sounded unsure.

"How was Dalton when he first got here?" Throwing a blanket over Brooks' back, I gave her ears a rub before adding the saddle and leaning down to cinch it.

"Distant. Wouldn't really talk about anything from the last few years and made a lot of trips out of town setting up new accounts."

Leading Brooks out of her stall, I looked toward my ex. "Sarah did the same. A completely clean slate, she called it. Deleted all her social media and changed all her accounts as soon as possible."

"One could say they were just starting over," Cody argued, saddle creaking as he swung up on Garth.

Following suit, I mounted Brooks, leaning to the side to adjust the stirrups. Because I was wearing sneakers and not boots, I needed them to be a bit higher than normal.

"One could say that," I agreed, echoing Cody's words. "But it seems to me like they were making sure no one could find them."

Riding out into the sunshine, Cody glanced over as I brought Brooks up next to Garth. Tilting his hat down, he waited a moment before answering. "Guess we're gonna find out."

Falling silent, we headed out, and if I closed my eyes, it felt like old times, when we'd been madly in love and would spend hours riding the range together. The time we'd spent together had seemed like minutes, and though much of our drama was public knowledge, few knew just how long the rancher and I had known each other.

Cody and I had first met at a rodeo. While he brought home bull riding trophies, I received my own prizes as both a barrel racer and a steer wrestler. Bull riding came soon after, and I won more than a few championships in a male-dominated sport. Our names became synonymous, and we became the rodeo world's favorite couple. Everything had seemed perfect, and when I'd decided to retire and use my cosmetology degree and open my own salon in Flamingo Springs, I'd thought life was mapped out. That is, until two months into our engagement when Cody broke things off, citing he didn't love me like he'd thought he did. It was a pattern that would repeat two more times, finally ending this past year once and for all.

Sighing, I brought myself back to the present and glanced at the man who rode in silence next to me. Breaking things off for good had been the best thing I could have done, but last month, Cody had asked me to take him back. Though he promised he'd changed, I couldn't help but feel bitter over the last several years of hurt he'd put me through.

Sensing my eyes on him, Cody looked at me.

"What?" His mouth turning up in a slight smile. "Got somethin' on my face?"

Shaking my head, I focused my gaze between the smooth spot between Brooks' ears. "No. Just thinking."

"About?" Cody pressed me, tugging on Garth's reins until

our horses were side by side and the toe of his boot brushed my calf. It was how we'd used to ride, holding hands and talking about raising kids and cattle.

My cheeks flamed. "Um, Dalton. Sarah. Everything that's going on. There have been four murders in a year. Flamingo Springs has been around for over forty years and never had a murder, and now here we are. One right after the other."

Scratching Garth's neck, Cody nodded in agreement. "Blaze said he ain't found anything yet on any of his leads. That's why I'm going out to the pasture. I can't just sit around and do nothing."

Falling silent again, we continued, and thirty minutes later, crested the hill that signified the beginning of the south pasture.

Bringing Garth to a halt, Cody stood in his stirrups, looking around, eyes crinkled at the corners as he searched for the plant he'd found in Dalton's truck. After a moment, he sat back down and clucked to his mount, and I followed him down the hill into the shallow ravine, Brooks bobbing her head when I gave her a soft whistle.

A few minutes later, Cody brought Garth to a halt again and swung down, letting the reins dangle loose. Dismounting, I patted Brooks' neck before joining Cody as he walked toward a patch of shrubbery that had partially climbed the young tree next to it.

Pointing, he said, "Winter honeysuckle. Highly invasive down here and a pest to trees and anything else it can climb. The previous owner of the ranch told me his great-grandmother brought the plant in. It's on my list to get rid of before it spreads too far."

"That's a shame." I studied the large bushes. "They must be beautiful when they bloom."

White buds dotted the thin limbs, and though they were

still hard fists not yet ready to unfurl, I could smell the sweetness of the blossoms.

"They usually don't bloom till late January," Cody said as he looked around the ravine. Twisting, he scanned the ground, forehead crinkling as he faced the sun.

Stepping away from him, I looked around, taking in the rolling green and brown hills that blurred into flat lands as I turned west. Clouds crowded the horizon, and after a moment of admiring them, I dropped my gaze to the ground.

Squinting, I saw a patch of dirt about twenty feet away slightly darker than the rest, and nudging Cody's shoulder, I pointed to it. "Think that might be what we're looking for?"

Elbow brushing my side as he turned, Cody looked to where I pointed. After a moment, he nodded. "Looks like it."

Grabbing my hand, he pulled me forward. After a moment of resistance, I followed him. The calloused hand that grasped mine felt both strange and familiar. I debated pulling away but knew he'd only done it from habit and meant nothing by it.

Once we'd reached the darker area of ground, we knelt together and studied it. With the sharp wind blowing every night, it couldn't have been too long since someone had overturned the dirt. After a moment, Cody released my hand, reaching around to grab his gloves from where he'd tucked them into the back of his pants. Slipping them on, he began digging at the mound of fresh dirt.

Just as I was about to stand, the cold from the ground seeping into my knees, Cody let out a triumphant mutter. The hole he'd dug was almost a foot deep, and the top of a plastic bag could be seen among the clods. Tugging on it, he lifted it out of the hole, almost dropping it when he saw what was in it.

"You don't think ..." My voice trailed off as we stared at the handgun in the see-through bag. Its dull grey finish gleamed in the white sunlight as Cody brushed dust away from the outside of the bag.

"Yeah," he responded grimly. "I'd say this is the gun used to kill Sarah, and Dalton was out here trying to find it."

Sitting back on my heels, I stared at the sober-faced cowboy next to me.

"Trying to find it? Or trying to hide it?"

The look Cody gave me was serious as he contemplated my words. Opening his mouth, he hadn't even gotten the first word out when the ground began to rumble, the sound of lowing and bellows reaching our ears.

Grabbing my arm, Cody jerked me to my feet as he shot to his, still holding the bag.

"Stampede!" he yelled as he ran toward our horses, dragging me along after him.

Reaching Garth, Brooks too far away for me to reach in time, Cody pushed me up into the saddle. He swung up behind me just as the first few cattle reached us, Garth stepping to the side as he did so, and Cody lost his grip on the bag.

Arms circling me as he grabbed the reins, Cody let out a piercing whistle, trying to herd the dozens of cows stampeding down the hill. Brooks was a faint shadow in the distance, having bolted moments before, and tugging on Garth's reins, Cody attempted to head in her direction as cattle ran over the bag.

"Grab onto my belt!" Cody yelled into my ear, fighting to keep Garth steady as cattle brushed against his sides, knocking my legs into Cody's.

Garth was an excellent herding steed, but we were caught in the middle of a stampede, and the usually steady horse lost his calm, pulling hard at the reins.

Reaching back, I hooked my fingers under Cody's belt and held on as he tightened his arms around me, Garth rearing up. Thighs burning as I squeezed them as hard as I could, I struggled to keep my weight toward the front of the saddle instead of completely on Cody's chest as he wrapped the reins around his fist, fighting to keep control of Garth.

Dust filled the air, sticking to Garth's sweating sides and coating the inside of my nostrils. A sudden sharp pain in my calf had me crying out as the horn of one of the cattle cut my leg.

"Cody!" Voice shrill, I tightened my hold on his belt until my hands cramped, blood filling my sneaker.

"Hold on!" Whistling again, Cody pulled hard on the reins, and I could feel him nudging Garth with his heels, trying to get the horse to move forward.

"Our best bet is to move with them until I can see a way out," Cody shouted. "They're startled, and I can't herd this many on my own."

Going with the flow, it was almost ten minutes before Cody was able to steer Garth through the herd and up a hill. After a moment, he leaned forward and pressed his hand against my calf, his other resting on my opposite hip. Garth's sides were flecked with white spots of sweat, and he stomped his hooves, still pulling on the reins.

"It don't feel deep enough to worry about bandaging it before we get back to the ranch." Pulling his hand away, Cody wiped my blood on my thigh. "And we'll need to disinfect it really good and have Jeff give you a shot to keep out infection."

"What about Brooks?" Twisting, I scanned the horizon, searching for my mount, shirt sticking to my back, my arms coated in fine dust.

"She'll head back to the barn." Several cattle still passed by, and Cody's chest heaved with a sigh. "I don't know how in the world that happened, but you can bet your last dollar it had something to do with us looking into why Dalton was out here. This pasture is fenced off for the winter. Only way those cows got out here is if they were herded and then spooked."

"Attempted murder?" I asked as Cody clucked his tongue and steered Garth in the direction of the house.

"Yep. And once we get your leg taken care of, I'm coming back out here to find that gun."

"If there's anything left of it," I mused, shifting, the saddle horn digging into my inner thigh. Looking around us, I scowled at the sight of the freshly trampled dirt. "How will you find the place where you dropped the gun? The ground is completely turned over from the cattle."

"I know," Cody replied, hand still resting on my leg. "But we were about thirty feet from the honeysuckle when I dropped it, so it shouldn't be too hard."

Removing his hand, he pulled his phone from his belt clip. "I'm gonna see if I got enough reception to call Greg and see if he knows what in the world is going on and have him get Jeff out here."

"I really don't think a shot is necessary," I protested, patting Garth's neck. His ears twitched back at the sudden pitch change in my voice. "It ain't hardly hurting anymore."

"Lacey," Cody chided me, chest warm against my back. "You've broken your arm twice and your collarbone, but you're afraid to get a shot?"

Shushing me before I could argue with him, he spoke into his phone.

"Greg? Get Jeff out to the ranch. We were stampeded, and Lacey's got a nasty cut on her leg. And find out who was assigned to the east pasture."

Hanging up, he clipped his phone back onto his belt and nudged me. "You all right?"

Nodding, I focused on Garth's mane. "Little shaken up, but I'm fine."

"Think you better back out of this and let me and Blaze handle it?"

The squeak my teeth gave as I gritted them was loud, and I

leaned forward so I no longer pressed against Cody. "Sarah was my friend and deserves justice, and I'm going to do whatever I have to in order to find out who's behind this. You got a problem with that?"

Chuckling, Cody wrapped his arm around my waist and pulled me back against him, our bodies swaying with Garth's easy canter.

"Nope. Can't say I do. But I want you to stick with me until we get it figured out. I want you safe."

I struggled to find a rebuttal to his order, but after a moment, gave up, staying silent. Glancing at our surroundings, I remembered the several rides Cody and I had taken through this pasture when we'd still been in love.

I gave myself a mental scolding. The past held nothing for me, and it was time to stop dwelling on it. Cody and I were done, and nothing was going to change that.

Shifting, I fixed my eyes on his house as it appeared on the horizon several minutes later. Jeff's truck was already parked in the wide gravel drive, his hound, Betsy, running circles around it with Luna and Henry, all three yapping loudly.

"Was it really necessary to call him out here?" I demanded, all eyes on me as we entered the yard.

Mason was leading Brooks into the barn as we crossed the drive, her sides glistening with sweat. Greg stood next to Jeff at the front of the doctor's truck, hands tucked into his pockets as he spit onto the ground.

"Lacey, you know as well as I do the bacteria that are on those horns. Yes, it was necessary." Cody's voice was dry.

"Whatever," I grumbled, sliding off Garth instead of letting Cody dismount first.

Doing my best not to limp, I made my way toward Jeff, ignoring the slight sneer that crossed Greg's face. We'd never gotten along since the first day we'd met, and the contempt between us had worsened when Cody and I had broken up for good.

"Lacey, I hear you got a nasty scratch from a horn. Care to take a seat in my office?" Giving me a crooked grin, Jeff lowered the tailgate on his truck and helped me up on it.

Behind me, Cody dismounted Garth, talking heatedly to Greg. "I want whoever was in charge of that herd up here now! They almost killed us, and it's gonna take hours to get that herd back in their pasture."

"I got Jake out looking for Tyler," Greg replied.

"Tyler?" Cody's voice rose. "That was his assigned pasture? He's second foreman, Greg. He better have a good explanation as to why he almost killed us."

"Pain level?" Jeff rolled my pant leg up as Aubrey rounded the corner of his truck, cradling two barn cats in her arms.

"About a four." I hissed through my teeth when he sprayed antiseptic on the gash.

"Lacey, what happened?" Aubrey's black hair was tousled from curious paws as a cat clambered up her shoulder. "I overheard Greg's phone call to Jeff."

"Never mind all that." My fingers wrapped around the cold metal of the edge of the tailgate. "Did you find anything out? We definitely found something suspicious before we were stampeded by a loose herd."

"I kinda got a little distracted." Aubrey worked a claw free from her shirt as the cat on her shoulder nuzzled into her hair. "Greg showed me the new kittens, and that's all it took for me to get off track."

"Not to interrupt," Jeff said, smearing ointment on my leg, "but Lacey, it's not quite deep enough to require stitches so I'm going to wrap it up and put you on an antibiotic. I do need to give you a shot, however."

"Do you though?" I scooched away from him. "My immune system is pretty tough."

Jeff pinned me with a look before digging through his bag. "Now, Lacey, don't make me stand here and tell you why you need it after all the time you spent in the rodeo. Don't tell me you're afraid of needles when you've been on the back of a 1,500-pound bull."

My retort was cut off by raised voices as Tyler entered the yard, Greg yelling as he followed him even as Mason tried to calm him down.

"Now wait just a minute." Tyler threw his hands in the air as he shook his blond head. "Didn't none of y'all get my messages? Someone cut the wires on the backside of my pasture, and I lost the whole herd. I've been asking for help for two hours while I rounded up what head I could find, but no one would answer."

"So why didn't you ride back here and get help?" Greg demanded, and Tyler rounded on him.

"Oh, I'm sorry, in-between repairing the fence to keep what cattle I could in and rounding up the nearby ones, it completely slipped my mind to waste time to ride back. Especially when no one would answer their phones."

"Everyone, calm down," Cody interrupted. "No one was killed or seriously hurt, so let's focus on rounding the cattle up and getting that fence fully mended. We'll find out who's behind this later. Might have some rustlers trying to move in. I'll contact Blaze and give him a heads up."

Greg's reply was cut off by my sudden yelp of pain as Jeff jabbed me with a needle full of antibiotics. Coming over by the truck, Mason gave me a concerned look, and I waved him away.

"The point is," Cody said, his voice much quieter now, several of his ranch hands gathering around him in a circle, "we all need to watch our backs. Rustlers are not something we take lightly, as everyone knows, and they have no limits as to what they'll do."

Faces grim, his employees nodded in agreement before

dispersing into groups, one led by Greg, the other by Tyler and Mason. It'd take several hours to round up the scattered cattle, and while Greg was busy doing that, Tyler and his team would be repairing the fence and looking for any traces of rustlers.

I glared at Jeff as he zipped his bag shut. "I didn't agree to a shot."

"I didn't ask." The doctor helped me to the ground.

"You two done?" Aubrey interrupted, the kittens playing at her feet. "We've got a case to solve, and standing around arguing over Lacey's fear of needles isn't helping."

"And playing with kittens is?" I lifted an eyebrow.

"It's good for my stress level." She smiled. "And I was thinking. There's no way one person was able to herd that many cattle. I know Cody is leaning toward it being rustlers, but I think it's whoever is behind the murders, and now we know there's more than one person behind them."

"Following that train of thought," Jeff slammed his truck door shut after putting his bag inside the cab, "that means no one should go anywhere alone."

"I agree." Cody rounded the front of the truck, Betsy on his heels.

I tugged on Aubrey's arm, jerking my chin toward her jeep. Henry was sprawled out next to the passenger door, Luna sniffing around his stretched-out legs.

"There's not much else we can do here," I said.

"Wait." She looked at Cody. "You told your ranch hands you think it's rustlers, yet you just agreed to my opinion it's the murderers. Which one is it?"

Crossing his arms over his chest, Cody pinned Aubrey with a hard look, sucking on his teeth. Blond hair tousled, jeans streaked with dust and some of my blood, he looked every bit the hardened cowboy he was.

"If there's anything I've learned in life, it's that you can't trust everyone. You should know that, Aubrey."

Aubrey's face darkened for a moment, and I knew her thoughts had turned to Mabel, someone she'd thought was a good friend who had turned out to be a murderer and had made several attempts to take Aubrey's life.

"One of your employees, then?" Jeff broke the silence, a kitten slowly climbing up his denim-clad leg.

"I'd hate to say it, but I wouldn't rule it out." Cody shrugged. "Sometimes people get tangled up in things they shouldn't."

The sudden chirp of his phone cut off the rest of his words, and he quickly answered it. "I'll let Blaze know," he said after a moment, eyes darting to mine. Lips twitching in what I knew was a sign of nerves, he ended the call and dialed Blaze's number while we watched.

The sudden wind that had come up blew sand into my face, and I licked my lips, grit scraping across my teeth. Aubrey shifted, her arm brushing mine, and we shared a glance.

"Blaze? It's Cody again." Cody dropped his hand to his hip, shoulders drawing inward. "The boys just found a gun I dropped when Lacey and I were stampeded. The bag it was in is completely shredded, but the gun is still in good shape, and they're heading back now with it."

"God help us," Aubrey said, one hand going to her throat.

"Indeed," Jeff agreed.

"Is that the suspicious thing you were talking about?" Aubrey asked me, and when I nodded, she closed her eyes for a moment and whispered a prayer.

Finishing the call, Cody turned toward us, his lips set in a grim line.

"No one leaves until Blaze says so. He's heading out here now with Chase. I'm gonna designate the front dining room as his interview room, so why don't y'all get situated in there while I call in the boys?"

Without waiting for us to reply, Cody turned away, thumb swiping across his phone screen, and I looked at Jeff.

"I am so tired of being interviewed." I sighed. "This is the fourth time this year."

Aubrey gave me a sympathetic look while Jeff pursed his lips.

"Gotta wonder when it's gonna stop," he said. "Seems like the last six months have been nothing but death and chaos. Not exactly what I'd wanted to tend to when I moved here."

"But there's been beauty too," Aubrey interjected as we walked toward the house, the dogs staying behind to tussle in the dirt, playfully yipping at each other.

Jeff looked at her curiously. "How so?"

Tripping slightly on a loose piece of gravel, Aubrey took a moment to answer, squinting up at the sky. "Blaze and I fell in love, for starters. And Brey met Kasey, and we gained him and Mitch as friends. Then Misty and Stetson finally got together, and Abby opened her toy store. And now with Cynthia getting clean and hoping to settle here in the spring and learn jewelry making with Jeni, it's clear there's beauty at the end of every difficult story."

"My mom always told me if things are bad, the story isn't over," I said quietly, walking between the dark-haired bakery owner and the tall doctor.

"I think your mom might be right," Jeff said after a pause, gesturing for Aubrey and me to step up onto the wraparound porch. Large green and red ornaments hung from the eaves, and I glanced at our reflections in them before reaching for the screen door handle.

Entering Cody's large home, I was enveloped with memories of us kicking off boots covered in dust from long days in the saddle. Walking down the hall and past the kitchen, I remembered all the times Cody and I had danced in it while old country played. That was where he'd proposed the third and final time, and my heart skipped a beat as I recalled how hopeful I'd been everything was going to work out.

Everywhere I looked reminded me of the plans we'd had. From the kitchen table where we'd spent hours dreaming of kids and cattle to the Bible on the bookcase filled with both our handwriting, there were memories of what had once been. "I wonder if the gun they found is the same one that was used to kill Sarah and Dalton." Aubrey sat at the dining room table, hands clasped in front of her.

Jeff waited for me to sit next to her before taking a seat across from us, stretching his legs out beneath the table. "I wouldn't doubt it."

"I don't know." I glanced around us at the cheery yellow walls and pine flooring. "Seems too easy to me if it is." Reaching forward, I fiddled with the drooping poinsettia. Cody had a habit of overwatering his plants, and this one was clearly no different.

"It does, doesn't it?" Jeff agreed while Aubrey nodded. Her lemon perfume scent drifted past my nose and mingled with the scents of Cody's aftershave, coffee, and whatever he'd cooked for breakfast.

"Thinkin' it was planted?" Aubrey scratched the side of her nose, dark eyebrows drawn together as she thought.

"Honestly?" I scowled at my friends. "That doesn't sound right either."

"Well it's one or the other," Jeff said. "Maybe whoever did it was panicked and thought it was a good place to hide it."

"And they weren't wrong. That was an excellent place to hide something," I said. "But they weren't careful enough when they did it, because Dalton was in that pasture looking around before he was killed, and I think he put the honeysuckle in his truck on purpose, so if something happened, Cody would know to check the south pasture."

"And you two were almost killed in doing so," Aubrey murmured.

The rest of her words were cut off by the rumble of Blaze's

truck as he rolled to a stop in front of the barn. The dogs' excited yipping filled the sudden silence when he cut the engine, and shoving my chair back, I went to the door, Aubrey right behind me.

Blaze stepped up onto the porch, his tall frame casting a shadow across the screen door. Cowboy hat tilted back, his green eyes were serious, but a smile played at the corners of his mouth when he spotted Aubrey.

"I sure am gettin' tired of interviewing y'all," Blaze said, opening the door as Chase tore himself away from petting the dogs and followed him. "Chase, go ahead and start the report. They should be back anytime with that gun."

Stepping back to let him enter the foyer, I chuckled. "And we're getting tired of being interviewed."

"Agreed," Aubrey sighed, face lighting up when the sheriff brushed a kiss against her cheek before gesturing for us to go back to the dining room.

The creaking of the floor in the hallway alerted us to Cody's presence. The ranch owner's hair was still mussed from our stampede adventure, and his lips were thin. Jeans and boots covered in dust, the muscles in his arm flexed as he shook Blaze's hand before sitting down next to me.

Taking the spot at the end of the table, Blaze took his hat off and set it on the table, the brim facing up. Dark hair pressed against his head, he looked younger than his thirty-some years, but one look in his eyes let me know the former Houston detective had seen more than his share of life.

"The boys will be back any minute." Cody clasped his hands on the table in front of him, thigh brushing against mine as he twisted to look at Blaze.

"Can I ask how well you know your ranch hands?" Aubrey leaned around me to look at Cody. Quirking a dark eyebrow, the baker's blue eyes were narrowed.

"I'm sorry." Blaze interrupted Cody's answer. "I must be

confused. Thought I was the one doing the questioning here." The look he gave Aubrey was stern, but she only rolled her eyes.

"It's all right." Cody cleared his throat, trying to distract the brewing argument between Blaze and Aubrey. "I know my employees quite well, and I trust every single one."

"With your life?" Aubrey pressed. "Or just in general?"

"Aubrey," Blaze warned, but she put her back to him, turning in her chair. Tired of having her and Cody lean around me, I scooched my chair back, Jeff giving me a sympathetic smile from across the table.

"I'd have to say in general," Cody answered. "I trust very few people with my life."

"So, it could have been one of your ranch hands who stampeded those cattle." A hard gleam came to Aubrey's eyes, and I wondered what my friend had figured out that I hadn't.

"Um, it's unlikely." Cody slouched in his chair while Blaze scrubbed a hand down his face.

"Interesting." Aubrey sat back. "Okay, Blaze, I'm done. Ask away."

"Thanks for your permission. I'll be sure to add you to the payroll."

His next words were cut off by the low chirp of Cody's phone, and he raised an eyebrow at the rancher.

"They're back." Cody shoved his chair away from the table.

Blaze stood. "While Chase is processing that gun, I'm gonna get a feel for who I want to interview first." Squinting down at us, he picked his hat up and placed it on his head, giving the brim a slight tug. "Think you two can stay out of trouble while I do that?"

Once Aubrey and I promised we would, Blaze left, Cody leading the way, and Aubrey gave Jeff a grin.

"What?" The doctor quirked an eyebrow, knowing full well

Aubrey's penchant for involving herself in police business. "What's that look for?"

"He only mentioned Lacey and me staying out of trouble. He didn't say anything about you."

"Now, Aubrey." Jeff raised his hands in the air. "I don't think I wanna get caught up in this."

"So don't think," I told him. "We'll take the heat."

Jeff paused and averted his gaze. He appeared to struggle with wanting to stay neutral but also wanting to join us. After a moment, a small grin came to his face. "Why not?" A gleam came to his eyes.

"Oh, good." Aubrey leaned forward. "Here's what I need you to do."

4

"I 'm not sure having Jeff snoop through everyone's things is a good idea," I cautioned Aubrey a few minutes later.

We stood in front of the living room window. Jeff crossed the backyard and entered the bunkhouse where several of Cody's employees lived.

"Please," Aubrey said. "Don't be a chicken. Even if someone catches him, they won't suspect a thing. Jeff is too much of a sweetheart for anyone to think he's up to something."

"I'm more worried he's going to find something." I kept my voice low.

In the dining room, Blaze interviewed Cody's ranch hands. The sound of Blaze's phone going off occasionally interrupted the low rumble of voices, and a chuckle filled the air as one employee left and another came in.

Even though it would take a few days for forensics to know whether or not the gun Cody and I had found was the same one used to kill Sarah and Dalton, Blaze moved forward as if it was. He warned each employee not to leave Flamingo Springs until he'd closed the case.

"Bunch of nonsense," Greg muttered under his breath as he

47

entered the living room, his interview finished. Bending, he plugged the Christmas tree in before checking his phone.

I studied him. Why was the foreman always in a dark mood? From the moment we'd met almost six years ago, he'd been surly, and his grim demeanor had grown worse over the years.

Crossing the room, he flopped down on the leather couch. Pulling his dip can from his pocket, he packed his lip, staring at me with hard eyes.

Greg and I had never gotten along very well, even when Cody and I had been engaged the first time. He'd always felt I was no good for his boss and had voiced it more than once.

"I know you're up to something."

Greg's sudden words caused Aubrey to jump, and she turned away from the window where she was still watching the bunkhouse.

"That a fact?" I challenged the scowling cowboy.

"It is." He hooked his left ankle over his right knee, one hand resting on the couch cushion while the other scratched the scruff on his chin.

"Fact or not," Aubrey interrupted, her voice even, "it's none of your concern."

Greg squinted. "You think you're untouchable now that you and Blaze are engaged, don't you?"

"No." Aubrey fully faced him. Her New York accent surfaced. "I thought that before I ever met him."

The sudden rise of voices in the dining room cut off my chuckle at her confidence.

"That's not fair, Blaze!"

Tyler's voice rang out as a chair scraped across the wood flooring. "Just because I was alone in that pasture in no way means I'm guilty."

"Now, Tyler," Cody said. "He didn't say you're guilty."

"And you ain't defendin' me," Tyler yelled. "I've worked for you for years, and this is how I'm bein' treated?"

"I'm not accusing you of anything. You need to calm down." Blaze's voice was level, and I shared a look with Aubrey.

"How can I calm down when you're telling me Jason found the missing pop socket from my phone case in that field where Cody and Lacey were almost trampled? I ain't been in that pasture since October, and I sure ain't touched no gun that don't belong to me." Tyler's voice rose again, and another chair scraped across the floor. "It looks like I'm the one who did it, and you're just waiting for the paperwork to process before you arrest me. I'm being set up!"

Greg came to his feet, face grim. "This ain't right." He stormed into the dining room as the rest of Cody's ranch hands left the front porch and entered the house to stand up for Tyler.

Aubrey turned back to the window. "Jeff better hurry up."

"And Cody better smooth this over before he has a walk out," I said. "Everyone loves Tyler, and if they think he's in trouble, they'll do whatever they need to in order to get him out of it."

"Gotta admit, his story has holes." Crossing her arms over her chest, Aubrey stretched her neck, giving me a quick glance before refocusing on the bunkhouse.

"I know. And maybe this is me being crazy, but it almost has too many holes."

Aubrey nodded while the men argued in the dining room, followed by a loud bang as someone slapped the table, making us both jump.

"For the last time," Blaze barked as Cody worked to get his employees under control. "You're not accused of anything, Tyler. But fightin' me this hard is starting to make me suspicious, so I suggest you calm down."

"Don't say a word," Greg warned his friend, his twang heavy. "Blaze is right."

Boots scuffed the floor as Tyler argued with his foreman before Cody separated them, sending his men back out to the porch so Blaze could finish interviews.

"Go to the bunkhouse and cool down," Cody told his second foreman. "You ain't in trouble. Take the rest of the day off and come back tomorrow with a better attitude. Got it?"

"Jeff!" I hissed at Aubrey, fumbling for my phone as Greg came back into the living room. The front door closed and opened repeatedly as the men trooped back outside, and turning, I watched as Tyler crossed the backyard.

Dialing Jeff's number, I did my best to look innocent as I muted the volume, Greg eyeing me as he sat back down. Scratching the bandage that peeked out from the edge of his collar, he cleared his throat.

"You look a little nervous, Lacey. Care to share?" Teeth bared in an intimidating grin, he pinned me in place with a suspicious look.

"I'm stuck in my ex's house with a smart-mouthed foreman. Yeah, I'm a little on edge." With shaky hands, I dialed Jeff's number again, resisting the urge to look out the window.

"You're not the type of woman to let something like that bother you." Moving his dip around in his mouth, he gave me another look.

"What happened to your neck?" I asked.

"Had an accident in the kitchen." Greg pulled his collar up to hide the gauze. "Tyler about had to use the fire extinguisher on me."

"I'm glad you're okay."

He nodded, then paused. "You know what?"

Aubrey sat on a leather chair that matched the couch, hands worrying the hem of her shirt. Sighing, she motioned for me to sit as well.

"I'm sure you're going to tell us," she said as I sat on the settee, sliding my phone into my pocket.

"I ain't seen Jeff in a minute. Makes me think he's in this with you two."

"In what?" Jeff's voice filled the room right before he stepped through the doorway that led to the den and the downstairs bathroom.

"Oh, nothing." Finally, I could breathe again. "Greg's just suspicious of everyone."

"With good reason, I'm sure." Jeff sat next to me and crossed one leg over the other. In the dining room, Cody let out a loud chuckle, Blaze and the ranch hand they were interviewing joining in.

"We're having way too much crime around here," Greg said. "I moved back here to get away from all the garbage that goes on in the big cities, and it's happening here too."

"I think that's why we all moved here." Aubrey folded her arms.

Greg blinked rapidly, perhaps surprised by the friendliness that filled Aubrey's voice. The two began debating the pros and cons of big city living, and Jeff nudged my leg with his. The scent of rubbing alcohol and hay wafted past my nose with his movements.

When I looked at him, he gave me a quick wink and nod of his head, darting his eyes toward the bunkhouse. He patted the lump in his pocket where he was obviously hiding something.

"Once Blaze gives us the all clear, we need to be heading back," he said, interrupting Aubrey and Greg's conversation. "Since we got dinner planned and everything."

Aubrey tilted her head to the side, then nodded before turning back to Greg and their discussion of New York subways.

"Lacey?" Cody stood in the doorway. "Blaze is about finished, and I need to talk to you before you go."

Pushing myself up from the settee, I winced as the cut on my leg pulled.

Cody wrinkled his brow. "You all right?" He stepped

forward as Aubrey shot to her feet. Reaching out, she steadied me as I wavered.

"I'm fine." I gave Aubrey a smile before looking at Cody. "What do you want?"

"Let's go outside." Cody gestured for me to go first and then followed me out to the front porch now devoid of ranch hands. He sat on a white porch swing and patted the spot next to him.

I gave him a long look before sitting. The December wind held the tiniest bite. Arms crossed over my chest, I leaned back as Cody pushed the swing back and forth with his foot.

Hands resting on his thighs, Cody let out a long sigh, and I glanced at him.

"Speak your piece," I said. "And it better not be what I think it is."

"It is. It's exactly what you think it is."

Facing him, I shoved a hand through my hair. "I'm not coming back, Cody."

"Lacey, I've changed." Voice full of emotion, Cody lifted one hand to touch my cheek. "And so have you. It would work this time, I promise."

Sighing, I stood. Cody's boots slid across the porch as he brought the swing to a stop before it could hit the back of my legs.

"You've said that before. Twice. And both times, you did the exact same thing. Wanted me to be committed but refused to commit yourself. I won't go through this again, Cody."

Cody stood, and his body brushed mine as he stared down at me, dark blue eyes wet.

"But this time, I'm telling the truth. Let me prove it to you. Let me show you I've changed. I've wasted enough time, Lacey. I know what I want now, and that's you and everything we'd talked about all those nights right here on this very porch."

"You promised we were going to focus on the case, not our

disaster of a love life." Taking a step back, I shoved an errant strand of hair behind my ear with a trembling hand.

"Well, watching Blaze and Aubrey makes it kinda hard." Cody tensed, as if about to step toward me, and I held a hand up.

"The answer is still no. And it'll always be no. I've given you as many chances as I can, Cody. At this point, I'd rather miss out on a life with you, than to go for it and always wonder if you're about to leave me again." I bit my lip as tears flooded my eyes. I still yearned to be with him. "It's better this way."

Cody looked at his feet, shoulders slumping. "I get why you feel that way. But you're wrong, Lacey."

The opening of the front door startled us, and I stepped back, right off the porch. I landed hard on the brown grass, the wind knocked out of me as pain made its presence known in my tailbone.

"Oh, my!" Aubrey ran down the front steps. The screen door smacked Jeff in the face as she let it go.

"Lacey, are you okay? I am so sorry!" Dropping to her knees, she reached for me right as Cody did, and the glare she gave the cowboy had him retreating.

Flat on my back, I stared at the bright sky, not sure if I should laugh or cry. It was only when Jeff's face appeared between Cody and Aubrey's I began to giggle.

"That had to have been a sight." I laughed but then winced as Aubrey helped me sit up and brushed dirt off my back.

"I mean," Jeff drawled, extending his hand and pulling me to my feet, "the whole windmill thing you did with your arms was pretty good."

"You all right?" Cody reached out as if to touch my arm but quickly pulled his hand back when Aubrey raised an eyebrow.

Brushing bits of grass off my pants, I grimaced. I'd have a good bruise in the morning.

"I'm fine. Didn't hit my head or anything, just my tailbone and my pride are all that are hurt."

Looking at Aubrey, I spoke over Cody's insistence I go back to the house. "We need to be going."

Not waiting to hear her answer, I walked toward her Jeep and ignored Cody's protests.

Once in the car, I turned to Aubrey as she shut her door. "I don't want to talk about it."

Turning the key in the ignition, she lifted her shoulders in a defensive shrug.

"I didn't say a word." Her mouth quirked to one side as she backed up. Turning the wheel hard, she slowly drove down the gravel drive. Soft Christmas music played on the radio.

"You didn't have to." I huffed and then settled back into my seat like a petulant child. "It's all over your face. Jeff's too."

Aubrey fiddled with the air dials before adjusting her sun visor, her movements quick and sure.

"I mean, he has some nerve, asking me to come back." I slid down in my seat and glared at the passing scenery, the house only a speck in the side-view mirror. "First, I gave Tom his engagement ring back and planned on focusing on growing the business with Sarah, and now Cody is determined to win me back for a fourth time."

"And I thought you didn't want to talk about it." Aubrey braked slightly before turning onto the highway.

"I don't. I really don't. My love life is one disaster after another."

"Well then, let's talk about the case. What do you think Jeff found?"

"No clue. But since we're all having dinner together tonight, I guess we're gonna find out."

"WHAT IS THAT?"

Nose wrinkled, I stared at the stained shirt Jeff had tossed on Aubrey's kitchen table. Dinner had been filled with talk of the case and the fight between Tyler and Blaze, and it was after we'd cleared the dishes that Jeff shared what he'd found in the bunkhouse.

"That, my dear lady, is a blood-soaked shirt I discovered hidden in Tyler's room." Jeff leaned back in his chair, toothpick between his lips.

"But whose blood?" I poked at the stiff shirt with my finger while Aubrey sipped a cup of tea. "And why not wash it? Or throw it away?"

"When Blaze found Dalton, his gun was on the seat next to him with a couple rounds spent. I think whoever this shirt belongs to was on the receiving end. They were grazed on the neck, as that's where most of the blood is." Jeff spoke around the toothpick. "Thing is, there's no way for Blaze to find out whose blood this is, as he can't exactly make everyone give him a blood sample without a warrant, and no one we saw today acted injured."

"Blaze didn't tell me about Dalton using his gun," Aubrey said quietly.

We fell silent for a moment, and I imagined Dalton trying to save himself. What must have been going through his mind in those last moments?

"But why keep the shirt?" I asked after a moment of sober silence.

Aubrey sipped her tea aggressively, muttering about Blaze not telling her things. "Maybe he was gonna plant it somewhere. And maybe, like Jeff suggested, that's not his shirt. That's an extra-large, and Tyler looks like he wears a size medium."

"Might've been planted in his room then. Or he's helping someone hide it." Face pensive, Jeff studied the dirty shirt.

"With all the holes in Tyler's story today, I don't doubt that. I think he's involved along with someone else." Aubrey quirked an eyebrow. "You know everyone on Cody's ranch better than any of us, Lacey. What do you think?"

"I don't think any of them are capable of hurting anyone." I shook my head. "But we thought that with Mabel and again with Seth." Frowning, I turned to Jeff. "Did you find anything else?"

"No. Just the shirt."

"We should give it to Blaze," Aubrey said, but Jeff pursed his lips.

"It's contaminated evidence now. I've touched it and removed it from the scene." Leaning forward, he picked the shirt up between his fingers and stuffed it back in his bag. "No, we've gone this far. Might as well keep going."

"Never thought you'd be one of us," Aubrey mused, studying the doctor. "Breaking the law and joining forces with the nosy women team."

"Yeah, well," Jeff chuckled. "It's keeping me busy."

"Any guesses on who that gun they found might belong to?" I propped my arms on the table.

"I bet it's registered as stolen," Aubrey said. "Only a fool would hide their own gun like that."

"Maybe not," Jeff countered. "Because they went through a lot of trouble to hide it and almost killed Cody and Lacey to try to keep it that way."

Aubrey pointed a finger at Jeff. "Good point."

Pushing away from the table, Jeff stood, picking up his bag.

"Think we should call it a night, ladies. I still need to finish some work at the clinic before I can head home."

"We need to get back to the ranch as soon as we can." Aubrey pressed her hands to the table and pushed herself up.

"Actually, we need to corner Blaze and find out what's going on." I pinned my baker friend with a look. "I believe that's your job."

Jeff let out a snort as he headed for the door. "Bribing an officer of the law, eh?"

"Better call Misty." I grinned. "She knows all about that from bribing Chase."

"You two," Aubrey fussed, picking up her and Jeff's coffee cups. "But you're right."

"Lock up after me," Jeff said as he opened the door. "Keep me updated, and I'll do the same."

Bidding the doctor goodnight, Aubrey and I quickly tidied her apartment before heading to bed. Settling down on the couch, I turned to my phone and pulled up an article on what was trending in the nail art world. It wasn't long before my eyes drooped, and I placed the phone on the coffee table.

As soon as I pulled the afghan to my chin, I was wide awake. The gash on my leg throbbed. My thoughts turned to the events of the day and to the young, second-in-command foreman.

Tyler had always been kind to me when I'd dated Cody and had continued to be that way even after we'd broken up. Quick to laugh, he was slow to lose his temper. The thought of him being behind our attack today and possibly the murders didn't sit well with me.

I snuggled down into the soft, worn cushions of the couch. As far as I knew, Tyler hadn't known Sarah, and since her and Dalton's murders were clearly connected, I doubted he'd had anything to do with them.

With Blaze tracking down Sarah's former boss in Florida and chasing every lead he could concerning Dalton, I found myself wondering why Sarah had been so determined to start over. And for that matter, why Dalton had been doing the same.

Blaze's angle was the two of them were hiding from

someone, and maybe they had been. His theory was they were victims. But perhaps, they weren't the victims after all.

Sarah had paid for everything with cash when she'd come to Flamingo Springs, and while my interactions with Dalton were limited, I'd never seen him use anything other than paper money.

I shifted, and the crocheted blanket slid down my chest as I struggled to make sense of my racing thoughts. It'd been a welcome surprise to hear from Sarah after all those years, and I'd shrugged it off as a thing of good fate. But maybe my old friend resurfacing in my life had nothing to do with fate and more to do with the fact Flamingo Springs had been popular on the national news the last six months, starting with Vicki's murder, then Ryan's. Perhaps Sarah had seen my name in one of the articles and realized my salon would be the perfect place to start over.

While Vicki's death had been the result of jealousy, Ryan's had been because of drugs, and Blaze and Stetson had found themselves up against a large drug ring from Houston.

The thought Sarah and Dalton might be involved in something as sinister as drugs disturbed me. I sat up, pushing the afghan to the side. Standing, I made my way to Aubrey's bedroom and knocked on the door. After she sleepily answered, I entered and sat on the edge of her bed.

"What's wrong?" she mumbled, her voice almost hidden by the sound of her fan blowing in the corner. "Is everything okay?"

"I don't know. This could probably wait until the morning, but I've got this thought stuck in my head, and it's bothering me."

Aubrey sat up and switched on her bedside light. Black hair in a messy braid, her eyes looked tired, and the ring on her left hand twinkled in the light. "Tell me."

I bit my lip. "What if Sarah and Dalton weren't really the

victims? What if they were criminals, and that's why they came here?"

Aubrey squinted at me, nose scrunched up. "What made you think of this?" She moved her feet so I could sit cross-legged on the bed.

"I'm not sure." I tapped my fingers against the soft afghan that covered Aubrey's bed. "I've been racking my brain ever since Sarah's death, trying to think of anything that might help Blaze, and that's made me analyze everything she said and did. There's so much that doesn't add up. Maybe Sarah was involved in something."

Aubrey rubbed her eyes. "It does put everything into a different light. And even though it's giving us even more questions, it might answer how Sarah and Dalton had so much money when they came here."

"You're right." Eyes widening a bit, I stared at my friend as she had the same realization I'd had only minutes before. "People who are on the run for their safety usually don't have money like that."

"But someone who's been participating in illegal activities would." Aubrey rubbed her chin.

"Dalton used to work for Cody back in college. Once he graduated, he moved home to Florida where he met Sarah, and followed her here to fix their relationship."

Aubrey huffed. "Or so he said."

"I was never close to him like I was with Tyler and a lot of the other ranch hands. But Cody was and so was Greg."

Aubrey frowned. "Then I think we know our next steps."

"We do?"

"Well, not ours. Yours." Aubrey grinned. "You need to get Cody alone and find out everything he knows about Dalton. Even the smallest thing could be what we need."

"I'm not so sure that's a wise idea. Every time he's around me he asks for another chance."

"Not much we can do about that." Aubrey stifled a yawn. "But he's not going to be willing to talk to anyone else and you know it."

"Very helpful." Scowling, I slid off the bed and winced as the cut on my leg pulled beneath its bandage. Placing my hands on the small of my back, I tried to stretch. Pain raced down my legs from my fall earlier that day.

"No use in worrying about it now." Aubrey slid down in bed and pulled the quilt back around herself. "Get some sleep, and we'll revisit it in the morning. Blaze should have more answers by then."

Bidding Aubrey goodnight, I made my way back to the couch and settled into my nest of blankets. This time when I turned the lamp off and laid down, sleep waited for me with open arms, and I didn't stir until Aubrey turned on the coffee pot the next morning.

"I called Cody while you were sleeping," she said, voice chipper as she moved around the kitchen, hair up in a neat bun. "You're having lunch at the ranch with him this afternoon."

I sat up, and my blurry eyes squinted in the light that poured through the kitchen window. "I'm doing what?"

"I did a lot of thinking after you went back to bed." Opening the fridge, Aubrey grabbed a container of leftover breakfast casserole. "Cody's holding something back from Blaze."

Back stiff, I slowly stood and stretched before folding my blankets. "About the case?" After I stacked the blankets and my pillow on one side of the couch, I padded into the kitchen and grabbed a coffee cup from the cupboard.

"That's my theory." Aubrey placed the casserole into a glass dish and slid it into the oven. "Not sure what it is, but watching him yesterday, I just got this feeling he knows something and thinks it's not important to the case."

"So why have me ask?" The coffee dripped into its pot. "Why not you?"

"I've a bakery to run and a wedding to plan." Aubrey leaned against the counter. "Your salon is shut down until further notice, so you've got all the time in the world."

"I feel like I could argue that point." I sighed as the coffee pot sputtered out a few last drops. "But it wouldn't do me any good."

Aubrey gave me a toothy grin. "Now you sound like Blaze when we argue."

After filling my cup, I made my way to the bathroom to get ready for the day. Thirty minutes and a cup of coffee and a shower later, I was almost done curling my hair when Aubrey knocked on the door.

Opening it, I raised an eyebrow as I twisted a strand of hair around the curling wand.

"Blaze just called." Aubrey crossed her arms over her chest. "The case is pretty much closed."

"What? Why? Ouch!" I flinched, shaking my hand after accidentally brushing it against the wand. "How in the world is the case already closed?"

"That gun you and Cody found? The serial numbers had been filed off, but not well enough, and they were able to trace it back to its owner."

"Tyler." My statement was backed by the whir of the bathroom fan, the scents of casserole and styling products swirling around us.

Aubrey nodded. "And I told Blaze about the bloodied shirt. He's getting a search warrant for the bunkhouse. Fussed at me about tampering with the scene but admitted the shirt would have been long gone by the time he got there."

"So if it wasn't planted, Tyler's going to know someone went through his stuff." I turned back to the mirror to spritz hairspray on my curls.

"I think Tyler's got bigger things to worry about right now."

"But what if his gun was stolen?" I grabbed a tube of mascara after quickly curling my lashes.

"Why didn't he report it? No one in their right mind wouldn't report their firearm had been stolen." Aubrey's voice grew quiet. "Tyler may not be guilty of murder, but he's tied up in this."

Dropping my makeup back into my travel bag, I turned to face my friend. "I know. It's just ... I've known Tyler for a long time."

"And I knew Mabel for years and considered her to be my dearest friend." Aubrey took a step back to let me exit the bathroom. "That didn't change the fact she was a killer."

We were silent as we dished up breakfast and sat at the table, both lost to our thoughts. To think Tyler might have possibly committed or was involved with not one, but two murders, was a hard thing to face, and I frowned as I forked cheesy potatoes into my mouth. The frown quickly turned into a relieved smile.

"So I guess you better call Cody and let him know lunch is canceled." Taking a sip of coffee, I savored the bitter flavor.

"No." Aubrey drew the word out, giving me a stern look. "That's not happening. I said the case is almost closed, not completely. There are still some loose threads, and I have more questions than answers."

I stared at my coffee cup. "Why me? Can't Jeni do it?"

Aubrey slowly shook her head. "Lacey, Sarah was your friend. Are you okay with not having at least a few answers?"

My friend's rebuke brought me up short, and I stared at her. My throat constricted.

"You're right. I need answers. And Sarah deserves it."

Aubrey nodded. "Exactly. So finish breakfast and come help me run the bakery for a few hours. It'll keep your mind busy."

Forking the last bit of casserole into my mouth, I stood and cleared the table. "I'm gonna spend every single minute trying to convince you not to make me talk to him."

Aubrey gave me a sweet smile. "And I'll listen. But I'm not changing my mind." She handed me her coffee cup. "You'll be fine."

Grabbing dish soap, I filled the sink with water.

"It's not me I'm worried about."

5

___

"I went through Dalton's will." Sitting across from me at the kitchen table, Cody wrapped his hands around a travel mug of tea. The stainless steel outside gave off a dull gleam.

"And?" I stared into his blue eyes and gripped the sides of my water glass.

Outside, the sounds of animals and a diesel truck echoed in the December air. The Christmas lights Cody had strung around the kitchen lent a cheery feel to the otherwise somber moment.

"States he wanted to be cremated. So I made the arrangements this morning."

"Sarah's said the same thing." I looked away. "Gone before they even really got to live."

"Life is short. And we only get one shot at it. No repeats. No second round. Makes you wanna not hold back."

Lips thinning, I gave my ex a warning look. "Don't even start."

"I had to try."

"And you failed. Move on. You know why I'm here, though

I'm sure Aubrey had you thinking otherwise." Words clipped, I took a loud sip of water.

"She tried." Cody chuckled, bringing his mug to his lips, eyes twinkling a bit. "But yeah, I know why you're really here."

"I don't think Tyler did it."

Cody put his mug down. "Thinking he did or didn't doesn't change the facts, Lacey. Between that gun belonging to him, where he was yesterday when you and I were almost killed, and the fight he and Dalton got into last week, it's just a matter of paperwork and a confession. Even if he ain't the one who pulled the trigger, he was part of it."

"What fight?" I leaned forward and rested my arms on the table. "No one told us about him and Dalton not getting along."

Cody shook his head. "'Cuz you ain't Blaze. Him and Dalton have never gotten along that well due to clashing personalities, but it came to a head last week. Greg and I had to get between the two of them, and I ended up with a split lip. Put both of them on unpaid leave for a few days and almost fired Dalton. If Jason hadn't stepped in, Tyler would have quit the same day."

"A fight doesn't mean Tyler murdered Dalton afterwards."

Cody pursed his lips. "It could when Tyler threatened to kill him after we broke them up."

"What was their fight over?" I took another drink of water, my socked feet cozy as they rested on the heated floor Cody had installed himself. "Surely not just because they didn't agree on something simple. Tyler's too even keeled for that."

Tan face drawn in the yellow kitchen lights, Cody ran a hand through already messy blond hair. "Not when it comes to protecting what's his." Wrinkles fanned out around Cody's eyes as he frowned. "And Dalton was a threat to that."

"I'm not following."

"Both Tyler and Dalton were involved in things they shouldn't have been." Cody's shoulders lifted as he sighed. "Tyler was in a gang when he was a kid and has worked very hard to get where he is now. It's not something he talks about, but he's got a rap sheet a mile long."

"And Dalton?"

"Dalton got messed up in stuff when he left the ranch. Spent a few years battling drug addiction and came here to dry out and patch things up with Sarah. Far as I know, he only ever bought and used, but that life has a way of trying to drag you back, and his old buddies were former friends of Tyler's."

"And Tyler felt they were coming for him." My voice was flat. Tyler very well could have murdered Dalton to protect himself.

"Exactly. Once a member, always a member, whether you want to be or not, and these guys will kill you if you try to leave."

"But that doesn't explain Sarah's murder." I pushed my glass of water away and drummed my fingers on the tabletop.

"It doesn't. Unless she was tied up in it too."

"Does Blaze know this?"

"No. Not the things about Dalton. That was between him and me."

"I don't think Tyler did it, Cody. I really don't. And you not telling Blaze about Dalton's past could be what puts an innocent man behind bars for life."

"Are you serious right now?" Cody's sudden flare of anger startled me as he set his mug down hard, tea sloshing over the brim and down the sides to pool on the table.

"They found his gun hidden in the field with the serial numbers almost completely sanded off. It's been proven it's the gun used to kill Sarah and Dalton, and he lied about where he was yesterday. I know you two were friends when we were engaged, but you need to face the facts." Cody's voice rose as he tried to cow me with a dark look.

"Excuse me?" My own voice took on a pitch of anger as I

half rose from my chair. "Face facts? I'm not the one withholding evidence."

"It's not important to the case."

I snorted. "Isn't that up to Blaze to decide?"

"Oh, please." Cody rolled his eyes. "Don't act like you haven't been snooping around and aren't holding stuff from him too. In fact, wouldn't this be your third time around doing that, since you and the girls think you're little detectives?"

I pointed my index finger at him. "We've never withheld something we thought was important. Which is what you're doing. Dalton is dead. He doesn't care about his reputation. Obviously, Tyler is involved somehow, but you're letting him take the heat for murder when he may not be the one who did it."

"There you go again." Hands pressed to the top of the table, Cody came to his feet in a smooth movement and leaned forward until our noses were almost touching.

"You always believe everything is neat, clean, and perfect. You refuse to accept things as they are and you live in a fairytale world where everything is okay. Face it."

Mouth falling open in shock at the sudden personal attack, I jutted my chin out. "And you always think you can do whatever you want and worm your way back into peoples' good graces just because you've won a few rodeos." Placing my hands on the table, I matched Cody's stance, fingertips burning as they touched the spilled tea. "And you don't care who you hurt, because at the end of the day, all you care about is yourself."

"At least I accept people for their flaws and don't insist on changing them to fit my narrative." Cody's voice dropped, a sign we were moments away from having a full-on fight.

"You're right," I said, tone even. "I insist people change when I see they're engaging in harmful behavior. I refuse to enable or tolerate that."

"Oh, so my behavior was harmful?" Cody's eyes narrowed. His minty breath fanned across my face.

A shiver went through me at the growl in his voice, and I had the urge to run out to my car and drive away as fast as possible. Instead, I stood my ground, drawing on an inner strength I didn't know I had.

"You can't stand here and pretend they weren't, but your actions almost destroyed me. And they did destroy *us*. So yes. Yes, your behavior was harmful."

Face softening, Cody's eyes glistened, and he looked down. "I know. And I'll never forgive myself for messing up the best thing I ever had."

Looking up, he leaned forward slightly, lips brushing mine as he spoke. I tried to pull back but found myself frozen.

"I still love you, Lacey Baker."

The last of his words were muffled as he covered my mouth with his, one hand coming up to cup my jaw.

The familiar warmth of his lips on mine, the way he stroked my cheek with his thumb like he'd done a million times before held me captive, and I found myself returning his gentle kiss.

Heart thudding in my ears, I lost myself in the moment. Feeling my surrender, Cody smiled, the movement breaking the tension, and I jerked back.

"You gave me your word we'd focus on the case."

"Don't pretend you didn't enjoy that." Cody's hand still hovered by my neck.

"Please." I shook my head, my movements small. "The only reason you did that is to distract me from what we were arguing about."

Cody shrugged. "If that's what you want to think." His eyes narrowed. "But we both know it's because our story isn't over."

Sitting back down, I took a long sip of water before answering. "Our story has been over for a while, Cody. And I'm not interested in rereading it. If you thought kissing me would get me to leave you alone about the case, you're dead wrong. You need to tell Blaze."

Cody stared at me for a long moment before grabbing a dishtowel and mopping up his spilled drink. I crossed my legs, shifting to one side. He locked eyes with me and moved toward me.

The intimate moment was interrupted by the sound of a gunshot, quickly followed by the tinkling of shattered glass from the kitchen window.

Diving forward, Cody landed on top of me, toppling my chair backward onto the floor. The wind knocked out of me, I could only stare into his worried eyes.

"Think you might be right about there being more than one person involved," he grunted. Rolling off me, he crawled across the floor.

Minutes later, as the front door opened, the air filled with shouting as ranch hands converged on the house.

"What in the world!" Greg's yell entered the kitchen before he did, pistol at his side, and I looked at him.

"Bit late to the game." Grabbing the edge of the table, I pulled myself to my feet. Whoever had just attempted to kill us was already long gone.

"That shot came from the east," Cody told his foreman. "Take some of the boys and see what you can find while I get ahold of Blaze."

Greg jutted his chin toward the hole in the kitchen wall above the microwave. "Were you sitting with your back to the window?"

Cody eyed the table where we'd been sitting. "I was." Eyes going from his chair to the hole in the wall, he paled.

"What?" I asked. "What's wrong?"

Lips pursed as he holstered his gun, Greg met my worried gaze. "That bullet wasn't meant for Cody, Lacey."

"Then who was it for?"

Greg's gaze flicked upward, and I finally understood.

"You can't be serious." One hand covering my mouth, I stared at him.

"He's right." Cody stepped toward me and tapped his phone screen. "If you hadn't shifted when you did, your blood would be splattered all over the wall."

"No." Knees weak, I sank into the chair next to the one overturned on the floor. My bruise from my fall the day before ached.

"Why would someone be after me? Out of all of us, I know the least."

Greg started toward the door as Jason entered the kitchen. "Apparently whoever just tried to kill you doesn't think so," he said over his shoulder.

"Get her out of here, boss." Jason rested a hand on my shoulder. "She's a target."

"Question is," Cody held his phone to his ear, "why?"

"Eat this. It'll calm your stomach down."

Blaze slid a peppermint candy across his desk. Cowboy hat pushed back, a strand of dark brown hair lay across his forehead. It lent a boyish look to the usually serious sheriff, and his green eyes were kind as they assessed me a few hours after my second near death experience.

"Thanks." I picked up the candy. Unwrapping it, I popped it into my mouth and let the sharp taste overtake me for a moment.

Blaze rested his hands on his desktop, and the computer in front of him made a soft whirring noise.

"With Tyler in jail, I thought I had a slight handle on the issue, but apparently not. And after what Cody told me about

Dalton, I have a feeling there are some things about Sarah you need to tell me."

I blinked. "Excuse me?"

Blaze stared. "Cody told me how hard you went after him to tell me what he knew about Dalton. Something about that hints you know more about Sarah than you've let on, even to Aubrey."

Tucking the mint into my cheek, I sighed, slouching in my uncomfortable chair. Hands shoved in the pockets of the thin hoodie I'd donned, I felt like a delinquent in the principal's office.

"I don't know anything." I stared hard at the small Christmas snow globe on the edge of the desk.

Blaze leaned back in his chair, and I glanced at him as he crossed his arms.

"I can wait you out. Very easily. So you decide how hard you wanna make this conversation." Blaze had been a cop for a long time, and the look he gave reminded me of just that. Breaking me down would be small change for him.

"Lacey, someone tried to kill you today. Anyone in connection with you could be in danger now. Cody, Aubrey, Brey, Jeni ..." His voice trailed off. "If you won't tell me to keep yourself safe, do it for them."

Shifting the peppermint to my other cheek, I pulled one leg up on the chair, the sound of the candy sliding across my teeth loud in the quiet room. The quiet murmur of Chase talking on the phone in the reception area faded as I focused on my friend.

"You know how Cody told you Dalton got into some trouble? Sarah was in the same kind back in beauty school. I did everything I could to help her, got her in rehab, and that was that. As far as I knew, she never ran with gang members, never sold, just bought and used."

Blaze nodded and jotted down a few notes on the legal pad

next to his keyboard. "Any particular reason you didn't tell me this right after her murder?"

I shrank back into the chair. "I didn't think it mattered. It's been ten years."

"Doesn't matter? People will wait a lifetime to get revenge." Blaze looked at me and twirled the pen for a moment before tapping it on the notepad. "Whoever took that shot at you was long gone by the time the boys got out to that pasture. But that don't mean they won't be back. They think you know something and want you silenced."

"And what am I supposed to do with that information?" I crunched down on the candy and shoved a hand through my messy hair.

"I'm sending you out of town for a while. I don't have enough detail here to keep you safe, and on top of that, even if I did, this is getting to be too big of a case for that."

"Please tell me you're not about to send me to Cody's ranch. You did that with Aubrey, and Stetson did the same with Misty. Both times, they almost got killed anyway."

Blaze quirked an eyebrow. "Nope, I really am sending you out of town. But you were partially right. You'll be with Cody. Just not at his ranch."

My stomach dropped. "You can't be serious."

Blaze slid another peppermint toward me. "I am. You leave in the morning. Cody has a three-night rodeo over in Greshing. Half the state of Texas knows about you two and the circus of a love life you had. No one will ever guess you're with him, and that's the safest place you can be."

"You have got to be kidding." My voice rose as I stood. One look from Blaze had me quickly sitting back down. "First off, I refuse to spend any more time around that man than I have to. Second, that's one of the biggest rodeos of the year in the entire country. Any of the contestants see me and not only will the entire rodeo world know I'm there, so will the state of Texas. Hardly sounds safe."

Blaze toggled his mouse, not even looking at me as he scrolled.

"You won't be spending more time than you have to. You'll be with him the exact right amount. And no one will see you. You'll be in his trailer the whole time."

Blaze gave a disapproving look as he scratched his scruff-covered chin. He took a sip from the mug next to his keyboard, frowned at it, and set it back down.

"I'd hoped you'd have more faith in me. I know how well known you were and still are in the rodeo world. You forget I was once part of that life too."

"Why not just put me in a safe house? Surely that's got to be safer."

Blaze clicked his mouse before standing. "I tried and was turned down. The state department doesn't think you're in danger." He rounded the desk and motioned for me to follow him. "I'll come with you to help pack your things. You leave in the morning."

"Of course I do." I stood and followed him. "Stars forbid I get any forewarning, let alone a say in the matter."

I walked down the hallway, arms folded. "Just what I wanted for Christmas. Stuck in a trailer with my ex-fiancé while some maniac is out there trying to kill me."

"Could be worse," Blaze said over his shoulder.

I snorted. "How?"

"You could be stuck with someone you aren't in love with. Now let's go. You've a rodeo to get to."

"You know I hate it when you put your feet on the dash." Cody scowled. The early morning sun reflected off his aviator shades.

Two hours into the six-hour drive to Greshing, and we'd already argued three times.

Stretching my legs out even farther, I crossed them at the ankles as they rested on the dash of his rig. A slight ring of dust appeared by the heels of my boots on the black interior, and I grinned. If I was going to be forced to spend the next five days with Cody against my will, I was at least going to have fun doing it.

"Ask me if I care." I rested my head against the back of my seat. Glancing over at Cody, I quirked an eyebrow. "Seriously. Ask me."

Cody gritted his teeth as he stared at the road, and the muscles in his jaw bunched. "You've spent the last two hours deliberately getting under my skin," he said, one hand on the steering wheel while the other rested on his thigh. "You've got one more chance, and then I'm locking you in the trailer."

"If you were hauling one of the horses, I'd be all over that," I shot back. "They'd be much better company."

"We're stuck together for the next five days. Do you think you could at least try to make this easy?"

"Oh, I'm sorry." I pulled my phone from my pocket and replied to a text from Aubrey. "I forgot how difficult this must be for you. Not like you're the one who's got a killer after them or anything."

I shoved my phone back in my pocket and stared out the windshield. The scent of coffee, breakfast bagels, and my perfume swirled around the cab. The tassel from Cody's high-school graduation cap still hung from the rearview mirror, and a photo of his deceased father was pinned to the sun visor. I knew if I opened the glove compartment, I'd find a pack of smokes even though he'd kicked the habit when we'd first started dating.

"Remember the time we wanted to save on money and decided to sleep in the truck instead of getting a hotel?" Cody's voice was quiet as he fiddled with the dials that controlled the air.

I chuckled. "Terrible choice on our part."

Cody laughed. "Or the night we ran out of gas, back when I had that truck that was more rust than metal?"

"Or the time we bought a pizza and had dinner in the truck bed and felt like we ruled the world?" Voice whimsical, I let out a sigh as I remembered all the times we'd shared together.

Cody glanced at me. "We had a good run of it, didn't we?"

Sighing, I slid my shades down my nose and looked at him. "We did. We really did. But all good things must come to an end."

"I disagree." Cody placed his hand on the console, palm facing up. "And I can tell you miss it. You miss rodeo life and being on the road, and if I'm not being too bold, you miss being with me. Still don't know why you had to leave it completely and only do the salon when you could do both."

"I was tired of seeing people get busted up. And I do miss it, but I needed to settle down and have some roots."

Cody waggled his fingers, and I stared at him. "Give me your hand."

After a moment's hesitance, I did.

Long fingers wrapping over mine, he squeezed my hand, the warmth of his skin soothing as he stroked his thumb over the top of mine. Slow country music filled the cab, and when he spoke, his voice was soft. "Lord, I ain't got even the slightest clue what You're up to. But You're in this. You brought Lacey into this situation, and I know You'll lead her through it. Be with us these next few days in a special way, Lord." Giving my hand another squeeze, Cody gave me a gentle smile before looking back at the road. "Close your mouth, darlin'. You don't want to catch a fly."

"Since when do you pray?" I asked.

"Since I got my heart broke, and I don't plan on stopping

any time soon." Jutting his chin toward the glove compartment, Cody went on, "There's a notepad and a pen in there. Grab it. I've got some ideas I wanna run by you about the case."

Letting his hand go, I obeyed and placed my feet on the floorboard. My mind still reeled over the fact my ex really had turned over a new leaf.

Clicking the pen open, I looked at him. "Let's start with Tyler."

6

"Do you know who you pulled?" I asked later that day as Cody and I feasted on cooler sandwiches at the small table in his trailer.

We'd arrived at the rodeo grounds a few hours earlier and checked in, connecting the trailer to the water and electric hookups before Cody went and registered. The rodeo didn't start until the next afternoon, but contestants were advised to show up the day before and get settled in. Rodeos this size often saw crowds of well over a hundred thousand, and contestants needed to be familiar with where to go during the show.

Cody nodded. "I pulled Mama's Prayers and Whiplash for the first night. Don't remember the next two nights. And I'm doing a few other acts as well."

I winced. "Mama's Prayers? I didn't realize that bull was still in the game. Didn't he break your shoulder last year?"

"Oh, yeah." Cody waved his sandwich in the air. "I forgot about that."

I forced a smile. "Of course you did."

Taking a bite of one of the cookies Aubrey had sent with us,

79

I drummed my fingers on the notepad between us. Filled with scribbles and half-finished thoughts, it'd been the source of our interest for the last four hours of the drive, even though every trail we'd chased had come to a dead end.

"Guess I know what I'll be doing every night while you're in the arena."

Cody swallowed before answering. "Every single person is a dead end, Lacey. What are we missing?"

"I don't know." I ran a hand through my hair in frustration. "And from what Blaze said when we called him, it's difficult to trace Sarah and Dalton. Outside of college or work, it's like they barely existed."

"Well, Jason said when he's got some downtime tonight, he's gonna go back through Dalton's belongings."

"I still don't think Tyler is the one behind the murders. Or maybe it's that I don't want to believe he's guilty."

"Even if he ain't the one who pulled the trigger, he's definitely involved. Guilty by association." Cody took a swig of water before going on. "Never picked up on any kind of animosity between the boys except for the tension between Tyler and Dalton, so it's hard to think one of them might be the killer."

"I just don't know how Sarah is tied into everything." I doodled on the notepad, moving the pen around cookie crumbs.

Gathering up our trash, Cody stood and padded into the small kitchen.

"Maybe she wasn't. Maybe she was an innocent person who was killed because of who she knew."

Pen freezing, I glanced at Cody. "That thought had never crossed my mind. Cody, you might be onto something."

Wiping his hands with a paper towel, the tall cowboy gave me a long look. "And that might be why someone tried to kill you, Lacey. They don't know what you know. They're just aware you were friends with Sarah and are trying to snip every loose end."

I shuddered at the thought of being nothing more than a piece of thread to someone.

Cody's next words were cut off by the chirp of his phone, and after looking at it, he grabbed his hat off the table and strode to the door. "One of my sponsors. Local news wants an interview," he said over his shoulder as he opened the door and made his way down the steps. "Don't know when I'll be back. Keep the door locked, and don't let anyone know you're here."

He was gone before I could reply, which was for the best, because it would have been sarcastic. After locking the door, I worked on cleaning the trailer and getting it ready for our four-night stay.

I was staying in the bedroom while Cody would sleep on the couch, and I smiled as I made my bed. There'd been a time when owning a trailer to take to rodeos had been a pipe dream, and now it was a reality.

Thoughts switching to the case, I sent a text to Aubrey, running Cody's idea by her, and when she didn't reply after five minutes, I put my phone back down and paced the trailer.

The Bible on the in-wall bookcase caught my eye, and I stared at it for a long time before turning my back to it.

The sounds of trailers being backed in and festival noise was a soothing roar, and stretching out on the leather couch, I covered myself with one of Cody's hoodies. Staring at the ceiling, I remembered the last time I'd seen Sarah alive, how unworried and at peace she'd seemed. The more I thought about Cody's idea, the more I began to think he was right.

Eyes heavy, I dozed off, the scent of his aftershave surrounding me as the week caught up with me.

IT WAS dark when I woke up, and I shoved the hoodie off before sitting up. The campground had quieted down, and my mouth was dry as I fumbled for the light switch behind the couch.

Head feeling heavy, I sat for a moment after turning on the light. Hands hanging between my knees as I perched on the edge of the couch, I tried to process the dreams that had filled my sleep, eyes aching in the dim light.

More memories than anything, I'd been transported back to the Miami beauty school where I'd first met Sarah. Both eighteen and fresh out of high school, we'd quickly become friends and had spent several nights dreaming about owning our own salons. While my beauty dreams had been put on hold when I'd gotten more serious about rodeo life after graduation, Sarah had continued to pursue hers.

Cradling my throbbing head in my hands, I thought of all the times we'd shared, the double dates and the many coffee-and-donut-fueled nights we'd spent studying for exams. I lifted my head and stared blankly at the trailer wall as a dull taste filled my mouth. Double dates. Sarah and I had gone on a lot of them, rarely with the same guys twice though, but one date I'd long forgotten about had come back to me in my sleep.

The college freshman I'd been seeing had brought along his friend to meet Sarah, and the two had hit off. The night ended badly though, when her date was arrested for assault charges after he refused to take her no for an answer.

Hearing a key turn in the trailer door, I came to my feet as Cody stepped inside. "Sorry." He pulled the door shut and quickly locked it. "Ran into an old buddy of mine ..." His voice trailed off as he stared at me. "What's wrong?"

"Greg." My voice was thick from sleep. "He's our missing piece. Or at least one of them. Cody, Sarah, and Greg dated back when we were in beauty school. He was arrested in the middle of their first date for assaulting her."

Cody took a step toward me. He removed his hat and carefully placed it on the table.

"How are you just now remembering this?"

"I had a dream." My voice took on a defensive note at the accusation in his tone. "And I heard she dated him behind my back, so it's not something that's stuck with me. Especially because I only met him once, didn't know his name, and didn't see him again until you hired him over four years later."

"Greg told Blaze he had no connection with Sarah beyond the few times he'd met her once she moved to Flamingo Springs."

"And Sarah never said a word about him either." I sat back down and pulled the hoodie into my lap so Cody could sit next to me.

Taking the hint, he sat, stretching one leg while he rested his arm on the back of the couch behind me.

"Maybe she didn't recognize him. It's been what, close to ten years?"

"Possibly. He did have a beard back then."

Leaning forward, Cody pulled his phone from his pocket.

"Still, I'll text Blaze and let him know. I doubt anything comes of it, but it's something. You remember anything else?"

"Hang on." I turned slightly so I could look at him. "Cody, Greg was arrested for assaulting Sarah. You really think it's nothing?"

"That was a long time ago. I ain't excusin' his crime, but that don't mean there was bad blood between them when she came here three weeks ago."

"Even if she didn't remember him, he remembers her. There's no way he doesn't." My voice was firm as I texted Aubrey. "You don't forget the person who put you in jail, especially when you end up dating them for six months after you get out."

"Well, text whoever, and let's call it a night, okay?" Cody's voice had an edge to it. "I've got a long day tomorrow and don't wanna be up half the night."

Slipping my phone in my pocket, I stood and glared down at him. "You know, it's in me to argue with how dumb you're acting right now, but I'm tired, hungry, and am stuck in this trailer for the next three days."

"I ain't acting dumb." Cody stood, towering over me. "I'm acting like I don't like you accusing my friend of something without proof."

I tossed his hoodie at him. "And I'm going to bed."

He stared at me. "Just like that?"

"Just like that." I moved past him to the bedroom, talking over my shoulder. "We'll talk about it in the morning."

Phone chirping, Cody stormed after me, standing in the doorway to prevent me from shutting the door. "No, we'll talk about it now." He glanced at his phone, his flushed face going pale.

"What's wrong?" I took a step toward him. "Is that Blaze?"

"Yeah. He said he's been running background checks on all the boys, and Greg's had been on hold because of some sort of system problem. It just came back."

Sitting on the foot of the bed, I looked at my ex, heart suddenly in my throat. "Did he say what's in it?"

Cody swallowed hard. "Well, you weren't wrong about the assault charges, but none of that matters now."

"I'm not following." Crossing my arms, I watched a shudder go through Cody.

Looking at me, my ex's eyes were wide. "Greg's dead."

"NOT A WHOLE LOT TO say right now." Blaze sighed an hour later over the speakerphone. "One bullet to the head, execution style. No casing, no prints, nothing."

"Where was he?" Cody's voice shook as he sat next to me at the table, and I wrapped an arm around his broad shoulders. Some of his tension left at my touch.

"Just outside the bunkhouse." Blaze's voice was grim. "A silencer was used, because four of your boys were in the area when it happened and didn't hear a thing. The dogs found him and alerted Jason."

"I'm coming home." Cody scrubbed a hand down his face. "I need to be there."

"I'd prefer if you didn't." The sound of Blake's radio going off in the background cut his voice out for a moment. "Whoever is behind these murders is going after anyone and everyone connected to Dalton and Sarah. Best thing is for you to stay there and keep Lacey safe until I can get the FBI to realize I need some serious help down here."

"How is there no trace?" I asked. "Are we dealing with a ghost or is someone lying?"

"Oh, someone's definitely lying." The chuckle Blaze let out was dry. "No doubt about that one. Too early to make a lot of calls, but at this point, I'm having the whole ranch put on lockdown. I've got backup coming from Houston. No one leaves until I've got answers."

Looking down at the text Aubrey sent, I replied before glancing at Cody. Eyes shut, the vein in his temple throbbed as he took a deep breath.

"I know you're right, Blaze," he finally said, pinching the bridge of his nose between his thumb and finger while his other hand reached out and rested on my thigh. "But those are my boys. That's my home. My brand. I should be there."

"I know." Blaze's voice was sympathetic. "But your safety is more important than anything else, Cody. I'm keeping this as quiet as I can and have a few favors to cash in with some news outlets so the public doesn't know for a while."

Ending the call a few minutes later, Cody stared blankly at the table.

"I can't believe he's gone. And I can't even call his dad and let him know until Blaze can get a handle on everything."

"I can't believe it, either." Tightening my arm on his shoulders, I pulled him closer, placing my hand on his where it still gripped my thigh.

"With Tyler still in jail, it's pretty obvious it wasn't him." Cody's voice shook. "I feel like I don't know any of my boys right now." The tears he'd been holding back during the call with Blaze fell to the tabletop. "Lacey, I just lost one of my best friends. Forever. And apparently, I didn't know him like I thought I did."

Rubbing his shoulder, I let out a deep sigh. "I know. But we're gonna find who did it, Cody. And everything is gonna come to light."

"And there ain't just a target on my back. It's on yours too." Cody groaned and shoved his hand through his hair.

"I know that. But aren't you supposed to be trusting God with all this?"

Cody gave me a dazed look, blue eyes bloodshot, lashes spikey with tears. "Lacey, you getting a bit of Jesus in your life?" The hope that filled his voice was mingled with grief.

I hesitated before shaking my head. "Nope. Just reminding you of what you believe."

"Thank you. And maybe one day, it'll be what you believe too." He turned, pulling me against his chest, burying his face in my neck. "This hurts, Lace."

The usage of his nickname for me pinched my heart, and I snuggled against him, rubbing his back as he cried.

"I know. And I promise, I won't stop until we've got answers."

7

"He's tall, he's handsome, and got a smile that'll melt ya' mama's heart. Four-time national bull ridin' champion and last year's bronc bustin' king. Ladies and gentlemen, coming in on the back of Whiplash is Cody Jackson!"

Eyes glued to my phone, I took a bite of my cookie as I watched the rodeo livestream. Cody was one of the headliners for opening night, and the roar that filled the stadium was loud as it came from both my speaker and outside the trailer.

The cameras panned out from being in tight focus on the chute Cody was in as the gate was opened, and Whiplash busted out into the arena filled with dampened dirt and sawdust.

One hand in the air, the other clutching the bull rope with a glove made sticky with rosin, Cody's black-and-green leather vest and chaps shone under the white stadium lights. His hat went flying as Whiplash kicked up his back hooves. Sweat rolled down Cody's cheeks as the camera zoomed in on his face for a moment. Remixes of popular songs blasted from the speakers mounted all around the stadium, and the bass rumbled in my chest.

"Three!" the crowd screamed as the bull rider proved once again why his den back home was filled with trophies. "Two! One!"

The buzzer sounded as the sportscasters whooped and hollered, talking over each other as they praised Cody's flawless technique.

Jumping off the bull's back, Cody landed hard and quickly rolled away before Whiplash could turn and trample him. A well-known rodeo clown ran into the area, distracting the massive black bull until Cody had cleared the fence, grabbing his hat along the way.

"Cody! Cody! Cody!"

The crowd's chants almost drowned out the sportscasters as they replayed the ride on the large screens above the bleachers. Cameras panned in and out of the crowd of over sixty thousand people. From young girls to buckle bunnies who flashed heart signs at the camera, to retired bull riders, everyone cheered for their favorite bull rider.

A collective groan filled the air when the camera paused on an older woman with wiry gray hair and a light-up garland necklace who held up a sign with Whiplash written on it. Clearly, she was rooting for the bulls to win tonight, and I could only chuckle at her mock sour expression.

"Look at that hold," one commentator said as Cody was rated for his performance.

The cameras went back to Cody as he downed a sports drink behind the chute, one hand holding his mouth guard. The awkward angle of the camera pointing at him made him laugh, fellow bull riders slapping him on the back.

Blue eyes glowing, he grinned, hat clamped on his head. Trickles of sweat made paths in the dust on his cheeks, and he said something to a rider next to him before answering a question the reporter shouted at him above the roar of the crowd.

"One of the cleanest dismounts I've seen in a while," another announcer said, voice booming over the arena. "I've seen better, but getting off Whiplash is no easy feat."

Shifting on the couch, I took another bite of my cookie, adjusting the volume on my phone, heart racing as I waited for Cody's score to be announced. A clown dressed as a cowboy Santa entertained the crowd as the score was calculated. He cartwheeled across the middle of the arena as he cracked jokes.

"And the score is," another voice said, the screens going black before bringing up Cody's headshot, "eighty-eight point nine."

"Yes!" I shoved the rest of my dessert in my mouth before pumping my fist in the air, almost hitting the cabinet above me.

Stretching my legs out on the cushion next to me, I cheered as Cody gave the camera a beaming smile as the crowd went wild once more.

It would be hard for anyone to beat that score. There was no doubt the ranch owner would be going home with another trophy and at least two more sponsorships.

My heart pinched as I thought about going home. Once Blaze gave me the all clear, I planned to renovate my entire salon, unable to bear the thought of going back to work with it looking the same as when Sarah had been murdered.

Cody had voiced the same thoughts at breakfast that morning, wanting to remodel the bunkhouse. Despite the white teeth he flashed at the cameras before they panned to the next rider, there were shadows in his eyes, and his lanky frame was tense.

A sudden knock on the trailer door startled me, and I dropped my phone. It skittered across the vinyl flooring and came to a stop under the table as the knock came again.

Holding my breath, I stared at the door. It gave a bit as someone tested the handle. Finding it locked, they knocked again. When no one answered them, I heard the crunch of gravel under boots as they walked around the trailer, and I slid off the couch, pressing myself to the floor.

"This is silly," I muttered to myself. "Probably a crazy fan looking for Cody."

The person circled the trailer a few times before leaving, and I grabbed my phone from under the table. No one knew where I was, so I knew my actions had been a bit extreme, but with three people murdered and Blaze faced with more questions than answers, it was better to be safe than sorry.

I checked the time. Cody rode again in about an hour, this time on the back of a bull who'd entered the scene less than six months ago.

The scent of smoke reached my nose just as shouts filled the air outside the trailer. "Hey! Get away from that trailer."

I scrambled to my feet as flames crackled by the front of the camper. I unlocked the door and flung it open. Grabbing the small fire extinguisher nearby, I jumped, skipping the steps and almost turning my ankle on the gravel.

A stout cowboy rounded the back corner as I pulled the pin on the extinguisher, and he ran past me, shouting as he went.

"Call the cops, that guy just set your trailer on fire!" He ran after the dark figure darting in and out of camping spots, jumping over chairs and coolers.

Coming to the front of the trailer where the propane tank was, I doused the fire around it, and the smell of gas mixed with the scent of smoke.

A small crowd gathered around as I put out the last of the flames before running forward and shutting the valve on the tank. The metal was hot to the touch, and I winced.

That was close. Too close. An explosion like that wouldn't have just killed me, but possibly several others. Whoever was behind it knew I was in the trailer and didn't care who they hurt to get to me.

"You okay?" Cowboys and cowgirls surrounded me,

rhinestones and buckles catching in the setting sun as one of them spoke to a dispatcher on a bedazzled cellphone.

"I think so." I studied my hand in the weak light. Blisters were already forming on my fingers and palm, and my stomach clenched. We'd been seconds away from a devastating outcome.

"We need to clear the area," one of the girls said, her blonde pigtails swinging as she directed people.

"Kane, you go after JD and see if you can catch the guy who did this. Maizy, go to our trailer and get the first aid kit. Dustin, you go to the gate and direct the cops here. Everyone else, don't let anyone get close. That tank is still hot, and we need to get clear of it."

She grabbed me by the elbow and led me several sites away to a picnic table as someone placed a battery-operated lantern on it.

"Name's Rosie," the girl with the pigtails said, opening the medical kit Maizy handed her. "But most folks call me Boss."

"Boss?" I stared.

She grinned. "Fits, don't it? I'm a firefighter when I'm not barrel racing and hog tying." The squint she gave me was slightly confused. "Lacey? Lacey Baker?"

I nodded as she treated my burnt hand, and I tried not to wince. "That's me."

"Wait." Maizy came back over from talking to one of the other girls. "*The* Lacey Baker? Like, the girl who made headlines for being one of the few female bull riders at the time? And not only that, but the only one to be bringing home as many buckles as the men?"

"Ouch!" I gritted my teeth, resisting the urge to pull away from Rosie as she slapped ointment on my hand before wrapping it in gauze. "Yeah, that's me."

"So why are you here? And not out in the show?" Maizy sat next to me. "You were one of the best."

Pulling my gaze away from my hand, I looked at the redhead who couldn't be a day out of high school. She reminded me of myself when I'd first joined the rodeo, her eyes still undimmed by the darkness that lurks just beneath the surface of rodeo life.

"I retired. Opened a salon and put my feet up."

"So why are you here tonight?" Rosie patted the back of my bandaged hand before letting it go and quickly cleaning up the mess she'd made. "Why come to the biggest rodeo in the state, one you used to headline, and be hidin' out in a trailer?"

"We lost him," Kane said, saving me from having to answer the awkward question. JD followed him, bending over and resting his hands on his knees as the portly cowboy tried to catch his breath.

"I tried best I could," JD gasped apologetically. "But he was too fast, and I lost him in the crowd."

"Thank you," I told him. "If you hadn't had caught him in the act ..." My voice trailed off, and I cleared my throat. "Well, we wouldn't be having this conversation right now, would we?"

The crunch of gravel announced the arrival of several local cops, and I was elbow deep in interviews when Cody showed up over an hour later, his final ride for the night over.

"What's going on?" he demanded as a deputy talked on the phone with Blaze, getting all the details from the case in Flamingo Springs.

"And what happened to my trailer?" His voice rose as he took in the partly melted front of the black camper, the area now well-lit by headlights.

"Oh, I'm fine," I said, waving my bandaged hand at him. "Don't worry about me."

Striding over, he grabbed me, arms looping around my waist. "Tell me you're okay."

"She just did, champ," Rosie called out, and I laughed, enjoying the blunt humor of my new friend.

"I'm okay, Cody," I told my ex, heart racing as he laced his fingers through my belt loops, keeping me close. "Trailer is too, beyond needing a new front panel and gas lines."

The scent of sweat and animals surrounded me as Cody stared down at me, eyes dark with concern. His words were cut off as the deputy walked toward us, boots crunching on the large pieces of gravel, his voice tired as he spoke with Blaze.

"Yeah, old buddy, I get your point, but from our standpoint here, it looks like a kid up to no good. Multiple trailers were broken into tonight, and this wasn't the only fire, so I think it's pretty unlikely Lacey was targeted."

Stopping, he scowled at the ground as Blaze said something, and I could hear the sheriff's voice rising as he chewed the city cop out.

"Well then, why don't you come and secure the scene yourself?" the deputy demanded, one hand going to his hip in frustration as the other cops milled around finishing up interviews.

Whatever Blaze said next had the deputy taking back his words, and I chuckled. Cody tightened his hold on me as he listened to the deputy end the call.

"Well," the cop sighed as he looked at us, "your friend back home seems to think you were targeted, and I'll admit, he may have a slight point. Right now though, we ain't got enough proof to back that up, so I suggest until we get this figured out, you two watch your backs and be careful. Don't go anywhere by yourselves and always have a plan."

He handed Cody a business card. "That's got the case number on it beneath my name. Reference that if you call."

"Much obliged." Cody let me go and shoved the card in his front pocket.

The officers left soon after, and I pointed a flashlight at the damaged area of the trailer while Cody inspected it. The crowd had dissipated after greeting Cody, and I'd exchanged numbers with Rosie and Maizy, the latter still starstruck while the former had hugged me tight and whispered encouraging words in my ear.

"Well," Cody muttered, rocking back on his heels as he studied the twisted paneling, "gonna cost a couple grand to get it repaired. The lines look good, but I'd rather we switch to electric heat until I can get a better look at them."

Standing, he brushed loose bits of gravel from his knees and took the flashlight from me. Still wearing his leather vest, his chaps were on a nearby picnic table, his hat next to them.

The campground quieted down as people readied for bed, worn out from the first night of the rodeo. All around us, window after window went dark, though everyone left their front lights on. A coyote yipped somewhere in the field behind the parking lot and was joined by others, the familiar sound sending chills down my spine.

Cody sat at the table, turning the light off, and I sat next to him, taking a sip of sweet tea from the bottle someone had handed me hours earlier. My jaw clenched at the sudden flood of sweetness, and I leaned my head against Cody's shoulder.

"Not exactly what I had in mind for Christmas," I sighed. "I should be in Virginia right now with my mom, making cider and looking at the album full of Daddy's pictures."

Cody wrapped an arm around my waist, the sleeves of his shirt still slightly damp with sweat. "And I should be elated I won tonight. Should be texting all the boys and celebrating, but I can't. Two are no longer with us, and the third is in jail. Jason's so busy holding everything down I hate to bother him."

"Oh, Cody," I whispered, turning and wrapping my arms around his middle as I cried. "This isn't real. This can't be happening. Not to us."

"It happened to Aubrey. Happened to Misty. No reason it shouldn't happen to us." Cody shifted, his other arm pressed against my upper back.

"But at least they had leads," I mumbled into chest, the Texas night air cold. "We don't even have the slightest clue. Our only lead was Greg, and he's dead."

"Actually, that's not true." Cody rubbed my back, the sound of camper heaters kicking in around us loud in the quiet night, the sky above slowly filling with stars.

"What do you mean?" I pulled away and looked at him. "Cody, we don't have a single lead."

"Aubrey, Blaze, and Greg were the only ones who knew where you were." Cody's voice was tight as he stared down at me, and his jaw tightened in the dim light. "And I don't think the first two told anyone."

"Well, who would Greg have told?" I pulled away from Cody and slid off the bench, cradling my burnt hand against my stomach.

"Not sure." After placing his hat on his head, Cody gathered up his chaps and the lantern. "But he told someone, and they followed us here. And I think that's why he told them."

"Whoa." I held up a hand. "You can't just go from defending him last night to sayin' he's behind the fire tonight."

"I had a lot of time to think last night. And I've concluded you're a loose end that needs to be snipped, just like Sarah was. Greg was mixed up in something. There's no way he wasn't."

"So then why he was killed?" I followed Cody to the trailer. "If he was behind Dalton and Sarah's deaths, who would be behind his?"

Cody gave me a serious look as he held the door open. "When I was gettin' ready to ride that bronc tonight, I thought about how Seth had recruited Ryan and Royce to run drugs for him and what happened when Ryan wanted out."

I stood in the kitchen. Cody tossed his chaps on the couch and then locked the door.

"He took out the middleman."

"Exactly. He took him out because he was replaceable."

"Meaning?" Grabbing the notepad from the shelf by the table, I scribbled down ideas as Cody took off his vest and added it to the chaps.

"Meaning I'm seeing some similarities between the case with Ryan and this one. We've got three murders on our hands. Up until Greg's murder, I was thinking he'd killed Sarah and Dalton out of jealousy because of what happened in college. But now with Greg gone, I'm wondering if it's not that and something much more serious too. Maybe more than one situation."

Rubbing his forehead, Cody stared at me. "Tyler has a rock-solid alibi for where he was when both Sarah and Dalton were murdered, and he definitely didn't kill Greg."

"Maybe someone shot Greg as revenge for Dalton and Sarah. If he's even the one who killed them in the first place." Nibbling on the end of the pen, I let out a sigh. "And maybe none of it is connected whatsoever."

Nodding, Cody moved past me and rummaged in the fridge. "There's always that possibility too. But we both know they're connected. Not sure how, and maybe we're dead wrong in our assumptions, but somehow, all three are linked together."

After a moment of silence, he pulled back from the fridge and handed me a container of premade salad and a package of yogurt. Amidst the tense silence, his stomach made a loud growl.

"How in the world can you be hungry right now?" I set the food on the table while he grabbed bottles of water and closed the fridge.

Cody shrugged, sweat darkening the sides of his gray shirt. "Beats me, but I am, so I'm gonna eat. You want anything?"

A knock on the trailer door interrupted my terse reply, and Cody quickly stepped forward.

"State your name." He motioned for me to step into the bedroom.

Ignoring him, I stayed where I was, shoulders relaxing when Rosie's husky voice filled the air.

"Came to check on Lacey," she hollered.

"More like she's nosy," Cody mumbled, looking at me over his shoulder and rolling his eyes. Setting the water on the table, he opened the door and let Rosie step up into the trailer, hands in his pockets while he studied her.

Ignoring him, Rosie pulled me into a hug. No longer clad in jeans and a long sleeve shirt, she wore flannel bottoms and a T-shirt, and tattoos covered her muscular arms. One was a stylist's hair clippers, and I wondered if she'd ever worked in a salon. Standing in something other than the dim light of sunset, I was able to get a good look at her. Piercings lined her earlobes. The blondeness of her feathered hair came from a bottle, brown visible by her roots, and I quickly amended my previous thought.

"You doing all right?" Grabbing my bandaged hand, she checked her work.

"I am, thank you." Gesturing toward the table, I raised an eyebrow. "You want a drink or anything?"

"Nah. Just wanted to check on you." She gave me a look of equal parts concern and curiosity. "Lot of people are wondering if you're performing tomorrow night. Rumors going around you're comin' out of retirement."

"She's not," Cody said, and I glared at him as he sat at the table and opened the salad. "And I'd appreciate it if not too many people find out she's here."

"Any particular reason?" Rosie crossed her arms over her firefighter shirt, the white emblem on it stark against her black tattoos. "Of course, I won't tell anyone, but I'm a little curious."

"There's a reason," Cody opened his water, not looking at her. "And it ain't no one's business."

"No worries." Rosie seemed unbothered by his rude reply. "I heard that cop tell you two to be extra careful, so I thought I'd let you know we'll all be keeping an eye on your trailer, and if we see anything, we'll tell you."

"Thank you," I told my new friend, shoving a strand of hair behind my ear. "If JD hadn't seen whoever started that fire, I wouldn't be here right now."

"We got your back," Rosie said. "You need anything, just holler and someone will come running."

After a few more minutes of small talk, she left, and after locking the door, I turned on Cody, scowling. "Can you be any ruder? Her friend saved my life and your trailer, Cody. And she bandaged my hand on top of that."

Shoving a forkful of salad in his mouth, Cody gave me a long look. After a moment, he twitched his nose, a sign he was thinking about what to say. After swallowing, he pointed the fork at me. "Someone tried to kill you tonight. Not me. You. They knew which trailer was mine, knew you were in here, and didn't care who they hurt in order to do it. Pardon me if I'm not too warm to anyone new right now."

"Rosie isn't the one who tried to kill me." I sat across from him and angrily twisted the cap off a bottle of water.

"Didn't say she was," he replied, blue eyes steady as they stared into mine. "But you're way too trusting of folks. Consider my rudeness as a balance to that."

I took a long sip of water before answering, knowing he was right but hating to admit it.

"Now I know how Aubrey felt when Mabel was trying to kill her," I sighed. "No idea why, no clue who, or when they're gonna try again."

We were silent afterward, and my mind drifted to a few months prior when Mabel had murdered bakery owner Vickie and had attempted to kill Aubrey. Cody had been framed in the process, and it was during the worst of the case that we'd completely parted ways.

I looked across the table at him. What would my life have been if we had stayed together and had worked through our issues? A brief smile touched my lips. We'd be exactly where we were right now. Eating late night dinners in a camper after a night of rodeo performing, arguing over something.

Screwing the cap back on my bottle, I stood. "I'm gonna go to bed. I'm getting a headache, and I want to talk to Aubrey for a bit and see if maybe she can make any sense of what's going on."

Absorbed in something playing on his phone, Cody only nodded, and I padded down the short hallway and into the bedroom. After changing into my pj's, I sat on the bed and called Aubrey, but after two hours of going over everything we knew, we admitted defeat.

"It's just ..." Aubrey sighed, the sound of the industrial mixer in her bakery kitchen loud. She was probably making late night Christmas cookies. "There's no one else to look at. Greg was the only lead, and with him gone, Blaze said it's like chasing smoke. It would make sense he murdered Sarah and Dalton, and I truly think he did. But who killed him?"

Pausing, she muttered something about butter, and I heard her rummage through the fridge. The mixing machine turned off as she shut the fridge, static filling the air. "Are you sure you didn't see something? Or maybe hear something when Sarah was with you that would help?"

One arm under my head as I lay on my back, I stared up at the ceiling, the lamp next to the bed casting shadows on it. "Not a thing. Sarah never said a word about anything except her dreams with Dalton and our plans for the salon. She acted like the biggest weight had been lifted from her shoulders and was very unbothered."

"Then perhaps our theory they were hiding from someone

and thought they were in the clear makes sense," Aubrey said. "I don't think they came to Flamingo Springs to hide from the law. They came to hide from some enemies, and apparently, they thought they were safe."

"She was completely unaware of being in danger," I said quietly, throat tightening as I thought of my friend. "That's the only thing that comforts me, you know. Knowing she didn't see it coming."

"Her boss spoke highly of her when Blaze talked with him. And every lead he had to that old job and having bad blood with it turned out to be nothing malicious. At least, that's what he was told."

The clattering of metal on metal filled my ear as my friend spoke, her voice soothing as I cried, tears sliding down my temples to dampen my pillow.

"And everything with Dalton just keeps coming up against a wall," I sniffled.

"Indeed," Aubrey sighed. "Look, you've had a long day, and we've went over the case three times, top to bottom. Get some rest, and we can look at it again tomorrow. Maybe by then, Blaze will have something."

"All right." I wiped my eyes.

Ending the call, I washed my face in the small bathroom, turned the lamp off, and crawled under the blankets. Surrounded by the scent of Cody's aftershave as he snored away on the couch in the living room, it wasn't long before I fell asleep.

8

"You've got to be kidding me. You boys are a long way from L.A."

Cody's drawl woke me up the next morning right before seven, and I sat up in bed as the trailer creaked, people climbing the steps.

"Nah, she's still asleep," he said in answer to a mumbled question, and after a moment of groggy confusion, I knew exactly who he was talking to.

Almost falling on my face as I jumped out of bed, I jerked the bedroom door open. "Mitch! Kasey!"

Running forward, I was grabbed up into a tight hug as the two YouTube stars laughed, Kasey's ever-present camera digging into my ribs.

"What are you two doing here?" I demanded after letting them go.

The duo had been visiting Flamingo Springs when Mabel had attempted to murder Aubrey and had been an integral part in helping solve the case. They'd quickly become a big part of our lives, and Kasey and Brey, Aubrey's full-time help at the bakery, had fallen in love.

"We were on our way to Flamingo Springs for Christmas and heard a case needed to be solved," Mitch said. "So we decided to stop here and see if there's anything we can do to help."

"And get some good footage of Cody for the vlog, of course." Kasey grinned. "Putting his face in the thumbnail of a video will bring in an extra five or six million views."

"Fresh eyes," Cody said from where he sat on the couch. Already dressed for the day, he nursed a cup of coffee. "Exactly what I prayed for last night."

"I do like the thought of being an answer to prayer," Mitch chuckled, sitting down at the table. Even though it was barely thirty degrees outside, the city dweller wore shorts, flipflops, and a sun-faded shirt. He shivered and rubbed his arms, giving me a quick grin.

"Has anyone done an in-depth social media dive on the people involved?" Kasey sat next to Mitch and opened the laptop he pulled from his bag.

Cody stared at them. "Done a what, now?"

Kasey glanced at me. "Lacey?"

Shrugging, I grabbed a cup from the shelf above the sink and filled it with coffee from the pot Cody had left on. "I know nothing about that stuff. I can barely work my phone."

"Same here," Cody echoed, and we grinned at each other. There'd been many times we'd gotten lost on the way to shows because we'd insisted on using a paper map instead of GPS, and neither of us were planning on changing our ways.

"Okay," Mitch said slowly. "You wouldn't make it a day in L.A."

Pecking at the buttons on the computer keyboard, Kasey shook his head, brown curls flopping over his forehead. "I'm sure Blaze has already done all this, but it'll help us get to know and remember everyone involved."

"How's Misty?" Mitch asked me softly as his friend typed

away. Seated across from him, I looked into his dark blue eyes, not missing the wistfulness that filled his voice.

"She's happy. Married now and still gone on her honeymoon."

"I knew Stetson had proposed." He looked down at his hands. "Didn't know they'd already tied the knot."

"No one did," Cody said from the couch. "They eloped."

Kasey laughed. "Sounds like something Misty would do."

Mitch let out a sigh, and I nudged his foot under the table, giving him a sympathetic look. There'd been a time when he and Misty had considered becoming a couple. Though he'd been the one to break it off, I knew a small part of him wished it'd worked out. Glancing over at Cody where he finished his coffee, I knew how he felt.

"While I'm scrolling through social media to see if there's anything to find," Kasey said, unaware of the current of emotions sweeping through the room, "tell me about the murders."

"Or rather, how they were carried out," Mitch added, seeming to give himself a shake.

Looking down at the table, I twisted my fingers together. The sip Cody took of his coffee was loud in the quiet trailer, and after a moment, I looked back up at my friends.

"Sarah was shot in the back of the head, as was Dalton." Licking my lips, I glanced over at Cody. "Greg, Cody's foreman, was killed the same way."

"All three were shot in the back of the head?" Mitch frowned. When I nodded, he slid the laptop away from Kasey and clicked a few keys. "From how silent it just got, I'd say you two hadn't put that together. All three victims were killed execution style. So it's all connected, no doubt about that."

I met my friend's eyes when he looked up from the laptop. Kasey reached over and tapped the mouse pad as they took notes.

"No. We … We hadn't realized that. And two were carried out with a silencer."

Getting up from the couch, Cody came and sat down next to me, placing his cup in front of him on the table. "Lacey and I found the gun used to kill Sarah and Dalton. We were almost killed in doing so. It was traced to my second foreman, and he's in jail."

"But no silencer was found?" Kasey's voice grew quiet.

"No." Cody shifted next to me. "Blaze said it was possible it was still out there with someone or lost in the pasture where we found Tyler's gun."

"Except Greg was killed after that, and whoever did it used a silencer," I said.

"Three murders," Mitch said, hitting another key on the laptop. "All carried out in the same manner." He looked up. "Did the victims know each other?"

I nodded. "Dalton and Sarah were engaged. Dalton worked with Greg, who used to date Sarah and had gone to jail for assaulting her in college."

Checking his phone, Mitch frowned before typing something else on the laptop. Whatever it was had Kasey raising his eyebrows.

"What time does Blaze get to the office?" Mitch met my gaze over the top of the computer for the second time.

I shrugged. "Around seven, I think. The salon opens at eight, and he's always there by then."

"What'd you think of?" Cody leaned forward, voice sharp.

"Nothing I'm willing to share right now. Not to offend either of you, but you're so close to the people involved you've overlooked a lot of things, and I'm wondering if Blaze has pursued any of them."

"Good chance he hasn't or doesn't have the time," I said, ignoring the storm cloud next to me. "He's getting no help from the FBI and is overwhelmed without Stetson to help him."

"Mitch, if you've thought of something, I think you should tell me." Cody's voice low, he propped both arms on the table, hands clenched into fists.

Mitch shut the laptop and gave him a long look. "Your reaction right now is why I'm not going to. Not until I've talked to Blaze, because it could be a wild goose chase, and there's no point in you worrying about it unless it actually is something."

"You think Greg murdered both of them." Cody's statement was quiet.

Mitch lifted his chin. "I think it's a good possibility. One I think you've already thought of and have pretty much decided is correct. You just don't like hearing it from someone else."

"If Greg murdered Sarah and Dalton, then who murdered him?"

"Word gets around." Kasey's cheerful voice grew serious. "An old friend of Sarah's, perhaps, or Dalton's. Murdered Greg the same way he murdered them as a sense of justice."

The silence that filled the trailer was thick, and I swallowed hard.

"Greg wasn't a killer." Sliding out from the table Cody stood, grabbed his hat from the couch, and left the trailer, slamming the door behind him.

Looking at my two friends, I lifted my shoulders in a shrug.

"When I brought up the idea Greg might have been the killer, he got upset then too. But I believe it's a reasonable thing to think and the only thing right now that makes sense. Last night, Cody agreed with me. Now, I think it's hitting him again that not only is his best friend gone, but he was also most likely a murderer. I don't blame him for getting angry."

"According to this website I'm on," Kasey looked up from his phone, "it can take up to a year to get your hands on a gun silencer in Texas. And just like with a gun, there's a record of when someone buys one." He ran a hand through his hair. "I wonder if Greg owned one, and if so, when exactly he got it."

"Blaze arrested Cody's second foreman, Tyler. His gun was used to carry out the murders, and we found a bloodied shirt in his things when we snooped in the bunkhouse." Rubbing a hand down my face, I let out a deep sigh. "I don't remember Aubrey's case or Misty's being this tangled."

"Partially because you weren't in the thick of it." Mitch gave me a sympathetic look. "And also, there was only one murder in those cases."

"Anything else you can think of that might help?" Kasey asked, and after a moment, I filled them in on Tyler's past.

Leaving the two internet stars to work their magic, I showered, dressed, and made my bed. Cody was still gone by the time I made breakfast and visited with my friends before they hit the road to Flamingo Springs, and I debated texting him.

"Be careful, okay?" Kasey whispered in my ear as he hugged me tight. "Don't trust anyone, and be on your guard, no matter what."

Fighting back tears at the worry in his voice, I nodded against his shoulder, the scent of his beachy cologne strong in my nose.

"We'll be praying," Mitch told me, and I thanked him.

How could God be anywhere near me when so much tragedy had happened and was still occurring? I knew God was good, and I'd been raised in a Christian home, but I'd lost my faith a long time ago. The few prayers I'd prayed in the last week had felt futile. If God cared, He sure had a strange way of showing it.

THE RODEO HAD BEEN under way for over two hours. Cody didn't come back until an hour before he was due to ride, only to grab his gear and phone charger. He held up a hand when I started to speak. "I don't want to talk about it."

"Fine. Take this is out on me. I can handle it. Not like it's the first time you've done that."

Mouth opening, Cody gave me a dark look. After a moment, he shook his head and left, and once a few minutes passed, I followed suit. I was no safer inside the trailer than outside, and because I was at the biggest rodeo in Texas, I might as well go see it.

Gravel crunching beneath my boots, I weaved through the campsites in the dim light of dusk. Recognizing me from my competition days, the employees at the ticket booth waved me through, and I made my way to an empty seat in the middle row of bleachers.

"He's a name you're about to get familiar with—on the back of Bad Times in Paso, a three-time bull riding champion— ladies and gentlemen, I present to you all the way from Brazil, José Pedreira!"

Sitting down on the cold metal seat, I glanced around as the young Brazilian exited his chute. His seven-second ride seemed much longer than that, and I could see why he was about to become a household name.

The smell of dirt, animals, popcorn, and everything in between filled my nose. The white arena lights shone bright as they bore down on the several thousand people crowded into the stands, reflecting off the billions of rhinestones that decorated the spectators' clothing.

Cheers and whistles assaulted my ears as the crowd went crazy over the bull rider, his black hair shiny as he jumped the fence while the bull was quickly roped and wrestled back into a chute. My ears throbbed as music blasted, drowning the crowd out.

I glanced at my phone. Cody would be riding in less than half an hour, and I shifted, my leg bumping against the young girl next to me. Apologizing, I tried to focus on the scene before me but struggled to concentrate. It'd been years since I'd been in a crowd of this size, and I'd always been the one in the arena, not the one in the stands. I struggled not to feel like I was suffocating.

Following everyone's lead, I jumped to my feet and cheered for the next rider that came out, a young man who had just been entering the rode scene when I'd been leaving it. Eyes scanning my surroundings as I clapped, I saw several familiar faces. Rosie was one of them, sitting a few bleachers down and to the left of me, and she waved, the barrel racing and hog-tying portion of the rodeo already over.

Eyes going back to the bull riders, I didn't notice she'd left her seat until she tapped me on the shoulder. Motioning for me to make room for her to sit down, much to the chagrin of the girl next to me, she gave me a wide smile.

"Surprised to see you here," she yelled into my ear, her words almost covered up by the roaring crowd around us. "Kinda had the idea you had to stay holed up in the trailer."

"I am," I yelled back, clapping in encouragement for the rider who didn't even make it two seconds on the bull he'd drawn. "But I'd rather be here than there, so here I am."

"That's JD." Rosie pointed at the next rider. His ride was short lived as well. Not rolling away from the bull fast enough once he hit the dirt, he took a good stomp to the ribs. He crawled out of the arena as the clowns did their best to distract the bull so that the riders could rope him, a paramedic meeting JD just beyond the gate.

Injuries, both mild and life-threatening, were a part of rodeo life. Having suffered a few myself, I was thankful the most I had to show for my time in the arena was a bump on my collarbone and a scar on my thigh. I knew several riders who had been hurt much worse, some now wheelchair bound while others had passed away.

"Eh, he'll be all right," Rosie said as everyone around us groaned at JD's misfortune. "Not his first time having that happen." The rest of her words were cut off by the announcers as they gave JD's score and introduced the next rider.

"And now, on the back of Widow Maker, one of the top riders of the last six years, he's wild, he's crazy, he's a champion—can I get a holler for Cody Jackson?"

Jumping to my feet, I cheered loudly, watching my ex's face as the camera zoomed in on him in the chute. Biting down on his bright green mouth guard, he gave a sharp nod to the men holding the chute gate closed. When the bell sounded, they pushed the gate open, and the massive bull bucked into the ring. Back hooves in the air, clods of dirt flew across the ring, and I could almost feel my own teeth rattle as Widow Maker spun before lunging forward, Cody's body whipping back and forth.

Rosie let out a sharp whistle next to me as the clock counted down to zero, but even after the buzzer sounded, Cody remained atop the bull. Immediately, I knew something was wrong even as the crowd went crazy with excitement.

"Something's wrong." I grabbed Rosie's thick forearm. "I don't think he can dismount."

Riders filled the ring, trying to rope the still bucking bull that got closer and closer to the fencing, and I knew if he got too close, Cody's leg could be crushed, or worse.

"Folks, we've got a problem," an announcer said, and the stadium fell quiet as Cody struggled to free his hand from his glove still stuck to the bull rope.

Widow Maker lunged toward the fence, and at the last second, Cody was able to pull his leg up, boot heel next to the bull's ear as they slammed into the metal. The bull did his best to crush Cody again, and that time, he slid too far to the other side of the large animal. Hand still trapped in his glove, he was dragged along, trying to climb back up with his free hand.

Riders circled the bull, one struggling to rope him while the other leaned down, attempting to grab Cody.

"Oh, my word. He's gonna be trampled," the woman behind me gasped, and below me, the elderly couple, who'd been yelling like crazy all night, prayed.

Sliding further down the bull's side, Cody's body twisted, and the pop of his shoulder dislocating was loud in the silent arena. After a moment, he was able to grab his stuck hand, jerking as hard as he could until it was finally freed from the glove. He fell to the damp ground beneath the bull.

I jumped to my feet and ran down the bleacher stairs the moment the hooves struck him, climbing the fence as the bull was roped. Clowns ran here and there, still trying to distract the bull from Cody as it snorted. Ropes taut, the cowboys struggled to drag the bull toward the open chute, calling commands to their horses.

Pain shot up my shins as I hit the dirt hard, almost falling on my face before sprinting toward Cody, medics running from the other side of the arena.

Reaching him first, I fell to my knees on the wet sawdust. "Cody, can you hear me?"

He groaned, blood pooling around him. Rolling over, he lay on his back, one leg drawn up as blood dripped from the corner of his mouth and the multiple abrasions on his arms. Black vest ripped, his chaps were streaked with more blood, and his blue eyes were dilated as he stared at the sky.

"Don't move," I told him as he tried to sit up. "You've got to stay still."

The medics knelt down just as he tried to sit up again, and one gently held him down while bull riders surrounded us.

"Call the hospital," a medic murmured into the walkie talkie velcroed to his chest. "Have them get a crash cart on standby and a transfusion ready to go."

Cody's blood now soaked the ground around him, and the

knees of my jeans were red from it, the large gash right above his belt bubbling as he breathed. He coughed, the blood dripping down his jaw foamy, and I clutched his hand as the medics prepped him for the stretcher board they'd laid out.

"Miss, I need you to get back," someone said.

Cody groaned, fighting to sit up again. "No," he gurgled. "She stays with me. Please."

The medics shared a look before nodding at me to stay put. The arena grew silent as they placed a brace around his neck before quickly tending to the worst of his wounds. Somewhere in the crowd, a child sobbed as they witnessed the horrors of bull riding.

"Look at his hand," one rider said as the medics carefully placed Cody on the stretcher. "All the hide's been torn clean off."

"They're trying to get the gear off that bull," another said. "Looks like it was tampered with. Think someone poured glue in his glove and all over the bull rope."

Their voices faded as I followed the medics out of the arena and to the ambulance backed up to the exit.

"Sit here," one told me, showing me a small seat, "and don't move."

The ride to the hospital was bumpy, and I sat belted in a back-facing chair as the two paramedics worked to stop Cody's bleeding and keep him awake.

"Stay with me, man," one said when Cody's eyes drifted shut. "Tell me about your girl."

Cody struggled to blink before speaking, his words slurred. "She's my fiancé," he managed to mumble. "Soon as you let me outta here, I'm gonna marry her."

"I'll make you a deal," the medic said, his pale blue shirt smeared with blood. "You stay awake, and I'll make sure you get out of the hospital faster than you can say yee-haw."

The ghost of a grin passed over Cody's pale face. "Deal," he whispered.

Eyes falling shut, his head lolled to the side as the ambulance slowed in the hospital parking lot.

"He's flatlining!"

The back doors of the ambulance were flung open, and I cowered in the corner as the trauma team pulled Cody's stretcher board out and placed it onto a gurney. Calling out codes and phrases that made no sense to me, they ran into the hospital.

The cement entrance was painted red and from the ambulance lights, and my eyes throbbed as I stumbled through the door.

"Miss, come with me." A nurse grabbed my arm and steered me away from the huddle of doctors and hospital staff who surrounded Cody's bed.

Jerking away from him, I ran forward, boots loud on the tile floor.

"Cody!" My scream was loud in the hallway, but no one bothered to look at me as they focused on him.

"Someone restrain her, please," a doctor shouted as he grabbed scissors and began cutting up the sides of Cody's pants.

The same nurse grabbed me again, and this time, I wasn't able to get away. Pulling me away from Cody's bed, he dragged me into a small waiting room and sat me in a hard chair.

"Please, you have to let me see him!" Tears ran down my face as I struggled to stand, but the nurse refused to budge.

"Sweetheart, you'll only be in the way. They're doing everything they can." Voice soothing, the nurse knelt in front of me, hands gripping the armrests to keep me from moving too much. His purple scrubs were bright against my blood-stained jeans, and after a moment, I stopped trying to push him away.

"I can't lose him," I whimpered. "He's everything to me."

Grabbing my shaking hands in his, the nurse squeezed them and gave me a gentle smile, teeth white against his ebony skin. "God's got you," he said, brown eyes looking into mine. "Trust him, sweetheart. He's got you, and He's got your friend."

An alarm went off outside the open door, and someone's shoe squeaked on the floor, the sound of a phone ringing almost covered up.

"We've got a pulse," someone called out.

"Let's get him into surgery," another said. "He's gonna flatline again. Someone call McGee and let him know we're almost there."

The rattle of the gurney wheels filled the air, then grew fainter. Even though I craned my neck to look out the door, the only thing I could see was a reception desk with a vase of wilting flowers and a small sign I couldn't read.

"Let's get you into the private waiting room upstairs." The nurse stood, and his cross necklace swung out from his V-neck scrub top. "And I'll check the lost and found and see if I can get you some clean clothes."

Standing, I grabbed his hand and gripped it as hard as I could.

"What if he dies? I ... I can't do this alone." Sobs shook my body as I panicked, and after a moment, the nurse pulled me into a hug.

"I'll stay with you the whole time. You're not alone. And no matter what happens, I'll make sure someone is with you."

Taking a deep breath, I pulled away, wiped my face with the back of my arm, and nodded.

I didn't know what the next few hours held, but I had to be strong. There was no other choice.

"MISS LACEY?" A warm hand shook my shoulder, jolting me from the restless sleep I'd fallen into on the hard couch in the waiting room.

"Mmph," I mumbled, trying to sit up.

Aaron, the nurse who had stayed with me, pressed a paper cup of coffee into my hands.

Taking a sip, I winced as it burnt my tongue but was thankful for the reviving flavor that had me opening my eyes the rest of the way.

The digital clock above the door showed 4:43 a.m., and I smacked my lips before taking another sip of coffee.

"Thank you," I whispered to Aaron. Swinging my legs off the couch, I planted my socked feet on the cold floor, my shoes under the couch. The sweats I wore from the lost and found were about two sizes too big and rolled up at the cuffs, but they'd kept me warm in the chilly room.

"He's about out of surgery," Aaron whispered back even though we were the only ones in the room, the lamp in the corner giving a soft glow to the fake plants scattered around us. A few worn Christmas decorations were spread out around the room, and they stirred as air began to blow from the vent in the ceiling.

"Oh, thank God." I set the cup on the table next to the couch. "Do they think he'll be okay?"

Aaron stood, stretching. "Tentatively, yes. He did flatline three different times, but he's relatively stable now."

"Oh, no." Pressing a hand to my mouth, my swollen eyes burned with tears. "And his injuries?"

"As far as I know, several broken ribs, a punctured lung, ruptured spleen, and his left hip is hairline fractured, as is his left leg. He lost all the skin off one hand, has a major concussion, and other cuts and abrasions." Aaron gave me a long look. "That cowboy is one tough man, but tough or not, he's been in the game long enough to know to wear a helmet.

The only reason his skull didn't break open was because the good Lord gave him a hard head."

"I know," I sniffled. "I was engaged to him three different times. Trust me, I know how hardheaded he is."

Grabbing my phone off the table, I checked my notifications. Several missed calls from Aubrey and Blaze, as well as Misty, Jeni, and Mitch. Two voicemails from Cody's parents caught my attention, and I quickly texted his dad. Rosie had sent multiple text messages, and after a moment's deliberation, I dialed her number.

"Girl," she said, answering on the second ring. "You okay?"

"Kinda," I replied, massaging the back of my neck. "He's about out of surgery. I don't know when they'll let me see him."

"They're thinking about shutting the rodeo down and canceling tonight," Rosie said, stifling a yawn, and I could hear her moving around. "What happened? I heard someone say his rig had been tampered with."

Across the room, Aaron flipped through a magazine. He'd probably gone off duty hours ago but had chosen to stay with me.

"Well, this place is crawling with cops," Rosie said, taking a slurp of something. "And from what I heard, a slow-drying glue was poured into Cody's glove and was mixed in his rosin. Couldn't let go of the bull rope and couldn't remove his hand from his glove."

"His hand is completely stripped of skin. Someone tried to kill him."

"I don't know what all you've gotten mixed up in, but you need to be careful," my new friend said, her voice grim. "Whoever is doing this doesn't care how painful of a death they cause."

Hanging up a few minutes later, I let out a deep sigh before looking at Aaron. "Why did you stay? Surely, you've been off for a while now."

The smile he gave me was gentle, the cup of water he held small in his big hands.

"I stayed because God told me to. I was going off duty right as you came in, and I heard Him whisper someone needed to stay with you until your friends get here. You're not safe. And even if you were, no one should have to go through this alone."

"God told you?" I asked skeptically. "Forgive me, Aaron, but that sounds like you're saying God cares about me, and I assure you, He does not. The last eight months of my life are proof of that."

"Because times are hard, you doubt the goodness of a God who sent His only Son to die a horrific death?" Aaron's voice was quiet. "Because your heart has been broken by others and by your own actions, you choose to believe God caused it?"

My shoulders stiffened. "Well, He sure could have stopped it."

Aaron chuckled, stretching his legs out in front of him as he touched the cross that hung from his strong neck. "In a perfect world, yes. But we lost that privilege the moment God kicked mankind out of the garden. If God dictated everything in our lives, He wouldn't be a loving Father. He'd be an iron-fisted ruler, a slave master, and we wouldn't love Him nor would we know the benefits of His mercy and grace. We would hate him."

"Freewill," I stated.

"Indeed. It's a two-sided coin if you ask me. We like it because we can choose to do whatever we want but despise it when life hurts us."

"And yet when we choose to trust God and live for Him, we're still hurt by the actions of others," I argued. "Because free will allows them to do so."

"But when you trust God, live for Him, and lean on His mercy, You find that while life still happens, somehow, you thrive instead of just survive." Aaron's eyes glistened as he stared at me from across the room. "You're still in the same storm, but the storm is not in you, whereas it would be if you weren't trusting the One who knew you before you were even conceived."

"Beautiful words," I said cynically. "But I find them hard to believe when Cody might not live."

"And when you find it hard to believe, that is when you dig your feet in and trust." Aaron let out a sigh. "Lacey, I watched you while you slept. You're one of the most conflicted people I've met, and even now I can see you struggling to let go of doubt. You want to trust God. So why don't you?"

"Because," I whispered brokenly, tears running down my face as I covered it, messy hair sliding forward and catching on the bandage on my right hand. "What if He hurts me like everyone else has? What if He lets me down? I can heal from people breaking my heart, but how would I heal from God breaking it?"

Vinyl chair creaking, Aaron stood and crossed the room, sitting next to me.

"Lacey, the One who created your heart will never break it. God will never leave you. He'll never let you down. He is for you and He is with you."

"I want to believe that," I sobbed as Aaron wrapped his arm around my shoulders. "I do, but I'm so afraid. Aaron, I'm terrified if I fall, He won't be there."

Tears dripped between my fingers, dampening the gauze wrapped around my hand, and after a moment, Aaron squeezed my shoulder.

"God, help Lacey's unbelief. Show her Your love, Father. Just as You sent Your Son during the darkest time, when there was no hope, no light, I ask You to send Your Spirit and allow Lacey to know You for who You are. Not for what man says You are, or what Lacey thinks, but in the fullness of Your glory."

The simple prayer sent a chill through me, and there in

waiting room 202 at barely five in the morning, I gave my life to Christ.

***

"He'll be in an induced coma for the next few days," I explained to Blaze over the phone later that day.

Back in the trailer, I stretched out on the couch with an icepack over my eyes.

"I'm only allowed to see him three hours a day right now, and once his parents get here, it'll be even less than that."

"Cody's a tough guy," Blaze said, voice soothing. "He'll pull through."

"I hope so," I sighed. "Watching him get trampled last night and knowing he flatlined a total of four times has me on the edge of losing it."

"I know," Blaze replied. "I'm trying to figure out if I want you back here or if you should stay put."

"I don't think it matters." Pressing the ice pack against my forehead, I leaned my head back on a pillow, the sounds of people bustling around the campground almost drowned out by the trailer fan.

"Christmas is staring us in the face, and I hate to think you'll be spending it there alone if we don't get a handle on this case." Blaze's voice cut out as he spoke to Terri for a moment. "I'm hoping we'll have this figured out before then, but I can't make any promises."

A beep on the phone alerted me to an incoming text message, and lifting the ice off my eyes, I stared at the screen. "Mitch just texted me. He and Kasey are coming to stay with me."

"Good." Blaze sounded relieved. "They've been a big help already, helping me track things down since I can't get any assistance, and Chase has been out with some sort of flu for two days."

"Did you see if Greg had purchased a gun suppressor?" I sent a quick reply to Mitch.

"I did." Taking a sip of something, Blaze coughed. "And he did buy one," he said, a hesitancy in his voice.

I removed the ice pack and sat up a little. "What aren't you telling me?"

"We did a gun powder test on Tyler. Came back clean."

"And Greg's?"

"Still waiting for the results. Labs are slow right now. But even if they come back positive, he was a ranch hand. Handling guns daily is common, so the test will prove nothing."

I put the ice pack back on my forehead. "But Tyler is ruled out. I knew he was innocent."

"Not quite. He's still being held for withholding information about a few things. But yes, he's in the clear for being the murderer."

I pressed my head back against the pillow. "So we're back to square one. No answers. Everything is pretty much a dead end."

"Exactly. I've got three murder victims, my main suspect one of them, and I don't even know how to figure the attempt on Cody's life into it all."

"Or if it's even connected to what's happening in Flamingo Springs."

"Oh, I have no doubt this is all connected. Thing is, it's like I've been handed a puzzle box with no pictures and only half the pieces."

Ending the call a few moments later, I laid the ice pack on the floor next to the couch and stared at the off-white ceiling. After a minute of quiet prayer, I searched through the contacts on my phone. Dialing a number, I took a deep breath.

"Lacey!" My mother's overjoyed voice filled my ear. "I was starting to think I wouldn't be hearing from you. You've drifted from me, baby." When I didn't speak, the lump in my throat stopping me, Mom's voice softened.

"Lacey? What's wrong?"

"Nothing." After Daddy's death, my mother's health had declined, and I couldn't bear to add to her stress.

"Is there something you need?"

We'd drifted apart in the last few months, as I was tired of always arguing over the same thing. I had no desire to move back to Virginia, nor did I wish to date any of her friends' sons. The first day or so of my visit would go nicely, then after, we'd start fighting, and I wasn't able to bear it anymore.

"Actually, I wondered if you remembered my friend Sarah, from beauty school? She came home with me for Christmas one year."

"Was she the one with the nose ring?" Mom's voice held a slight tone of disapproval.

I chuckled. "Yes. That was her."

"I do remember her. Her sense of style was in desperate need of help, but she was an incredibly sweet girl." Mom's voice took on a hint of nostalgia, and I knew she was probably thinking of the days when Daddy was still alive. "That was the year your dad accidentally set the tree on fire."

"I'd forgotten about that." I rubbed my forehead. "Didn't the cat's tail catch on fire too?"

"Sarah helped him put it out." My mother continued as if I hadn't spoken. "And she became excellent friends with one of the male firefighters, if I recall."

"Tony," I said. "Nice kid. Is he still around?"

"Far be it from me to ask my almost thirty-year-old daughter what's going on," Mom muttered, "but you're asking an awful lot of pointed questions."

"Nothing I can tell you right now, Mom. But would you happen to have a way for me to contact Tony?"

"I suppose," came the slightly perturbed answer. "But if I

give it to you, I want an update on your dating life. You know I want nothing more than to hold a grandbaby in my arms before the Lord calls me home."

"Of course," I sighed. "Always a price with you."

"Nothing's free, sweetie. Not even when it comes to your mother."

"So you tracked this fireman down, and he told you what?" Sitting across the table from me, Rosie took a bite of chili. She'd arrived at the trailer right after her slot in the rodeo with a pot of steaming beans and tomatoes as well as a tub of ice cream. The police had decided to allow the rodeo to run for its final night, and the roar of the crowd was loud outside.

"That he'd lost contact with Sarah after a few years but she called him about a month before contacting me." Spooning a bite of the spicy food into my mouth, I briefly closed my eyes, savoring the explosion of flavors on my tongue.

"Did he say what she wanted?"

I swallowed. "She asked if he'd pay for two bus tickets and said she'd pay him back. He said something in her voice let him know she was in trouble, so he did. The trip was from Florida to somewhere in Louisiana. Never called him back, but he got an envelope not too long after with cash in it that covered the tickets."

"It sounds like she and her boyfriend wanted to leave no trace of themselves," Rosie mused, adding a spoonful of dill relish to her chili. Her blue shirt brought out the hazel in her eyes, the palm tree tattoo on her neck almost hidden by her chandelier earrings.

"Exactly. She disappeared from her job, shut down all her social media and bank accounts, and it's like she never existed. Far as Blaze has been able to tell, Dalton did the same thing."

"So why Flamingo Springs?" Rosie pointed her spoon at me. "Why you?"

"Sarah knew she could trust me. And Dalton knew he could trust Cody. Flamingo Springs is a great place to disappear, after all. It's why the spa does so well with all the celebrities and Misty's counseling appointments are booked out almost a year in advance."

Appetite gone, I stared down at my bowl.

"They went through all that, and still weren't safe. I just don't know how they were found when they'd both been so careful to erase themselves from society."

"Easy. The killer did exactly what we're doing now. Connecting the dots." Rosie took a swig of water. "My word, I made this a tad spicy. My eyes are starting to water."

"Are you saying I'm one of the dots?" I asked, my own mouth on fire after eating a hot pepper, my sense of smell momentarily gone.

"Yes. Somehow, this person knew about Sarah's connection with you and traced her to Flamingo Springs."

"But what about our theory Greg killed Sarah and Dalton?" I argued.

"Maybe he got to them first," Rosie suggested.

Burying my face in my hands, I let out a groan.

"If Greg did murder Sarah and Dalton, why? And who killed him? But most importantly right now, why is someone coming after Cody and me?"

"Your guess is as good as mine, honey." Reaching across the table, Rosie tapped one of my hands. "Hey, let's have some ice cream and just chill out, okay? The more we think about this, the more confused we're gonna get. I believe the answers will come to us when the time is right and not a moment sooner."

I lowered my hands. "I'm doing a terrible job at being a detective. My friends Misty and Aubrey are so much better at it."

Gathering up our bowls and setting them on the counter next to the crockpot, Rosie shook her head. "We all have different gifts. And from what you've told me, both of your friends had lawmen next to their sides the entire time. You don't."

Standing, I helped her wash the dishes before we filled two bowls with peppermint ice cream and sat back down at the table.

"True. But with Mitch and Kasey coming back to stay with me until Blaze decides what's the best next step for me, I feel a lot better. They were a big help when everything happened with Aubrey."

"Hopefully, they are again," Rosie said, spooning the sweet treat into her mouth. "Because you need all the help you can get."

9

"Help has arrived!" Mitch crowed as he and Kasey climbed the stairs into the trailer later that evening.

Almost midnight, the campground was quiet, save for the sound of generators running, a cold wind having stirred up. Rosie had long since gone back to her camper, and after touching base with Cody's parents, I'd been left on my own.

"Hope you're not tired." Kasey sat down at the table. "Mitch and I are hyped up on energy drinks and think we might have a good lead for this case after spending the day with Blaze."

Sitting across from him next to Mitch, I clasped my hands together on the tabletop. "Anything would help at this point. I feel like I'm going crazy."

Mitch stretched his arm out on the cushion behind me, the heat kicking in and blowing a warm gust across our feet.

"Social media is forever." He cupped my shoulder with his hand. "That's where we started. Sarah and Dalton did a great job of deleting everything, but Greg? He was terrible at it. Everything he posted lines up with him being the murderer."

"He registered to buy a gun suppressor a little over a month ago." Kasey drummed his fingers on the table. "In the state of

Texas, it can take up to a year to be approved to purchase one, and he was approved in less than two weeks. Posted about it all over his social media."

"That doesn't mean he killed anybody. Lots of people own a silencer."

"That is true." Kasey held up a finger. "And a suppressor, or, silencer, as most people call them, can be used on pretty much any gun."

"And I'm supposed to do what with this information?" I asked, a little cranky from the long day.

Ignoring me, Kasey went on. "Guns have calibers. And a silencer has a list of what caliber gun it will work with. The silencer Greg purchased? It wouldn't fit any of the ones he owned."

"It did, however, fit Tyler's." Mitch's voice was low. "A gun he said was stolen, yet he never filed a police report about it."

"A gun that had the serial numbers almost, but not quite, filed off so it could be traced back to him," I finished.

"Exactly."

Mitch dropped his arm and turned to face me, eyes gleaming.

"When Blaze confronted Tyler with that tidbit today, he admitted Greg had asked to borrow his gun. He had no reason to believe Greg had anything malicious planned, though why he'd let someone borrow his gun in the first place is beyond me. When Sarah was found murdered, he knew Greg was behind it, but was afraid he'd be charged with the crime because his gun was used."

"And that's where the bloodied shirt Jeff found comes in. Tyler got into a fight with Greg, and Dalton got involved. He heard Greg say he'd hidden the gun in the south pasture and went there to prove Greg was Sarah's killer. The blood on the shirt most likely belonged to all three men, and that's why Dalton looked beat up when he was found."

"And the few shots Dalton got off before he was killed?" Kasey said softly. "They found at least one mark. Greg. He had a bullet burn on his neck."

"But why didn't Dalton call Blaze when he found out?" I whispered. "Or when everything started to go down? He might still be alive if he'd gotten help." Nauseated, I bent forward and pressed my forehead against the cool tabletop.

"Just take a breath," Mitch said, rubbing my back as Kasey stood and went to the fridge. Coming back a moment later, he pressed a cold water bottle against the back of my neck.

"Dalton wasn't thinking straight." He sat back down, the table shifting with his movements. "Tyler said he swore he'd find that gun and see Greg in prison."

"So what now?" I asked, lips brushing the table as I spoke, the taste of bile strong in the back of my throat. "What happens to Tyler?"

Mitch cleared his throat. "He's been charged with being an accessory to crime and withholding information as well as a bunch of other things. It doesn't look too good for him. There were so many times he could've come forward, and he could've helped prevent Dalton's death."

"But what was Greg's motive?" I whispered, lifting my head and staring at Kasey as tears ran down my cheeks. "What did he have against Sarah? Against Dalton?"

"Revenge," Kasey replied quietly, not meeting my gaze. "Blaze wasn't supposed to tell us this, but ... The police were finally able to get into Greg's phone today. There was a secret file on it that took up several gigabytes of space.

Greg had written thousands of pages about Sarah over the years, and when she showed up in Flamingo Springs along with Dalton, he started writing about how he wanted her dead. One entry read she deserved to be murdered for leaving him all those years ago. Another entry included his plan to murder Dalton for being the one Sarah had chosen to spend her life with. Greg asked to meet Sarah at the salon before it opened under the guise of having a surprise from Dalton, and she fell for it."

"So who killed Greg?"

My question hung in the air for a long moment, and I twisted the cap off the bottle of water. The sharp movement pulled on the bandages that covered my blistered hand, and I winced.

"We don't know," Mitch said. "Maybe a friend of Sarah's, or Dalton's, but they worked so hard to disappear from the world, it's unlikely anyone even knows they're dead."

"And on top of that, who's after you and Cody?" Kasey added. "Neither of you saw the murders."

"I think Sarah had witnessed something," I told my friends. "She said her job ended badly, yet her boss spoke highly of her. It's been a theory of Aubrey and mine that she and Dalton either saw something and were on the run, or they committed a crime and were hiding."

"Cutting ties," Kasey said slowly. "And with how many murders and attempted murders there have been, I'd guess the former."

"Maybe this person thinks Sarah told you something." Mitch took the bottle from me, my shaking hands spilling water down the front of my hoodie.

"Well, she didn't. Everything seemed perfect."

"Two murders are solved, though." Mitch patted my shoulder. "We'll get to the bottom of Greg's murder in no time. I promise. Kasey and I prayed about it on the ride here, and I believe God's gonna give us the wisdom we need."

"I hope so," I said, doing my best to keep the doubt from my voice.

"Let's call it a night," Kasey said after a moment. "I'm exhausted from how much we've been on the road, and I'm sure you want to see Cody as soon as you can tomorrow."

After discussing the case a bit longer, we retrieved Mitch's suitcase from his vehicle and made sure everything was locked up. Once the two internet stars were settled in on the couch and on the bed the table folded down into, I slipped into the bedroom.

Laying down, I crossed my hands over my stomach, listening to the heater, the security light from the camper next to us shining around the edge of the blinds.

Greg and I had never gotten along, but not once had I ever suspected he could be capable of murder. With Tyler caught up in this mess, I wondered how many more of Cody's ranch hands knew something but were lying.

Turning on my side, I brought my knees up to my chest, suddenly cold.

I felt much safer now Mitch and Kasey were with me, but I couldn't shake the feeling we were all in danger. Whoever had killed Greg was determined to silence Cody and me, and I found myself fearing for my friends' lives.

"God," I whispered into the slightly chilly air, the electric furnace struggling to heat the camper, "please keep us safe. Help us to figure this out before anyone else is hurt."

After a long moment, I added to the simple prayer, remembering the words Aaron had whispered to me in the hospital waiting room. "Help me to trust You so that while I'm in this storm, the storm isn't in me. Amen."

Peace settled over me, and it felt like I'd only just fallen asleep when my alarm went off the next morning. Quickly showering and dressing, I made breakfast for everyone before climbing into Cody's truck and driving to the hospital. Mitch and Kasey stayed behind, having some work to finish for their YouTube channel.

Once the nurse allowed me into Cody's room, I pulled the visitor chair out from the corner and across the floor next to him. An IV slowly dripped at the corner of his bed, and I held his hand, careful not to disturb the multitude of wires connected to him.

The low beep from the monitor to my left matched the slow rise and fall of Cody's chest, and I squeezed his fingers. Bruises and scratches covered his face, and his injured hand, heavily bandaged, lay across his stomach. His blond hair was still stained with blood, the nurses unable to properly clean him up. Normally tan cheeks pale, he looked small, and my throat ached with unshed tears.

Cody and I had gone through a lot together, and despite all the heartache we'd put each other through, I could look back on those years with fondness. The good more than outweighed the bad, and no matter what, we'd always have each other's backs.

The night Cody had won his first national championship had also been the night he'd proposed to me the first time. We broke it off six months later, tried again soon after, and two months after, the ring had been back on my finger. Back and forth we'd gone, our relationship seeing epic highs and catastrophic lows, and in the in-betweens, we'd seen other people, yet somehow always came back to each other.

It didn't escape me that this time things were different. Cody had found God, and I was trying to do the same. Somewhere in the last six months, we'd both changed, letting go of the things that had gotten in the way, and the future, though blurry, seemed bright with promise.

"Please be okay," I whispered to the man who still held my heart, no matter what my mouth had told him. "I still love you. Still want everything we dreamed about and were working toward."

A sudden noise at the door interrupted my whispered plea, and I looked up as Cody's parents slipped into the room.

Luke and Danae had always been kind to me, keeping in contact even when I'd broken things off with their son for the final time. Getting to my feet, they pulled me into a warm hug, Danae rubbing my back as Luke kissed the top of my head.

"He's gonna be okay, Lacey," Danae whispered as I cried into her shoulder, the warm scent of roses and jasmine surrounding me. "The doctors said he'll pull through and should make a full recovery."

"You just cry it out, honey." Luke tightened his hold on me. "Lord knows we've done the same."

"He still wants to marry me," I sniffled, hair hot on my neck. "After everything that's happened between us, he still wants to call me his."

"Of course he does. The boy knows a good thing when he sees it. Might've taken him three more tries than your average man, but this time, he's got it right."

"The police called us this morning," Danae said as I stepped back from Luke and wiped my eyes. "His gear was definitely tampered with, and they're going through all the security camera footage to see if they can find anything. The videos aren't very hopeful, though, as there's so much activity around the chutes. It'd only take a quick second to douse his glove with the glue, and everyone they've talked to said they didn't see anything."

After spending a few more minutes with who I hoped would one day be my in-laws, I left the hospital, relieved Cody wouldn't have to be alone anymore. I spent the thirty-minute drive back to the campground in deep thought as I turned Danae's words over in my mind.

Whoever had attempted to burn down Cody's trailer and tampered with his gear had to be someone able to get close to him without him noticing. At least a dozen other trailers and trucks in the park looked just like his, and to sabotage his glove, the person must have been right next to him.

Frowning, I switched lines and passed a slow-moving car. Whoever was behind Cody's attack had to be involved in the rodeo. There was no other way they could have gotten that close to his gear. And with him now in a hospital surrounded by nurses, he would be safe from anymore attempts on his life.

A sudden chill down my spine had me cranking the heat up in the cab.

With Cody out of the way, at least for the time being, there was only one other person for the killer to fix their eyes on. Me.

The thought had me pressing down on the gas, eager to get back to the safety Mitch and Kasey offered. A cheerful carol played on the radio, and with a jolt, I realized the holiday was right around the corner. Nothing about the last week had felt joyful or bright, and I could only hope a Christmas miracle was on its way.

***

"ALL RIGHT, guys, that wraps up today's video. Drop a comment below and make sure you get involved with the community. We love hearing from you and can't wait to see you next time."

"That sounded good," I told Mitch as he and Kasey put the finishing touches on their latest vlog while I gave myself a manicure. Bright red with cheery Christmas trees painted on them, they brought a touch of color to what seemed to be a dreary world.

"Views are at an all-time high." Kasey pecked away at his laptop. "It's a great time to make some extra bank."

"I know what you mean," I sighed, applying a clear topcoat to my nails. My blistered hand cramped as I awkwardly held the brush, and I winced when a blister broke open. "I was booked completely solid this week with some of my biggest tippers. Lost all of that the morning Sarah was murdered."

A knock on the door interrupted Kasey's answer. Mitch opened it, and Rosie stood outside. Her dark green trailer was the only one left in the park besides ours, Maizy having been picked up by her parents the night before.

"Cookies, anyone?" She stepped into the camper and extended a large plastic container. "Probably ain't as good as Aubrey's, but they're not too bad."

"How do you know about Aubrey?" Mitch gestured for Rosie to take a seat at the table before sitting next to me on the couch.

"Oh, I've stopped in Flamingo Springs a time or two and had breakfast at her diner. Her peppermint mocha-stuffed cookies are fantastic."

"She just released that recipe about a week ago." I held my bottles of nail polish while Mitch twisted the caps onto them.

"Hmmm." Rosie pursed her lips. "Maybe I had those somewhere else."

"Must have," I agreed. "Aubrey will be disappointed to hear that. She thought she was the only one who'd come up with that recipe."

"Any plans for the holiday?" Mitch asked the firefighter, green eyes bright as he studied her.

Rosie shrugged. "Not really. Christmas isn't my cup of tea. What about you? Y'all staying until Cody gets released?"

"Until the sheriff back home decides what's safest," I answered. "With a killer still on the loose, it's hard to know what the right move is."

"Think that's safe?"

"That's why Mitch and Kasey are here," I said. "For protection."

"And entertainment," Kasey mumbled.

"That too," I giggled, gently waving my hands to dry the nail polish.

"So firefighting." Mitch leaned forward, hands clasped between his knees. "That always been your dream?"

"No," Rosie answered, seemingly unbothered by Mitch's

sudden interest in her personal life. "Actually, I was a hairdresser for a few years."

"I wondered about the shears tattoo on your arm," I interrupted, gently blowing on my almost dry nails. "Where did you study?"

"South Hall," Rosie replied. "Great school in Miami." She stretched, tone nonchalant as she glanced at me.

"Me too," I told her. "We must've shared a few classes together, as you're only a year older than me. Why'd you leave cosmetology and become a firefighter and barrel racer? Pretty much everyone who went to South Hall either landed high-paying jobs or opened their own salons, myself included, though I did compete in the rodeo for a few years first."

Rosie leaned back, crossing her legs beneath the table. "Well, I've always been in the rodeo scene. Born and raised on a dirt-poor farm and rode pigs before I could walk, but as for hairdressing? That was my momma's dream, not mine. I'm too rough and got too much energy to stand around a chair all day shooting the breeze. I need to be on my feet and be busy."

"May I ask where you were a hairdresser after you graduated?" Mitch's voice was light, but when I glanced at him, his jaw was tense.

"And can I ask why you're interrogating me?" Rosie demanded, uncrossing her arms, her own tone accusatory.

Mitch's lips turned down. "Oh, because I find it interesting how you just happened to be in the area every time something has happened to Lacey and Cody. And because it's Christmas, and for some reason, you're staying in an empty campground instead of going home."

"Mitch!" I glared at my friend, mortified. "Rosie, I'm so sorry. Please ignore him."

"It's okay." Rosie held up a hand, eyes hard as she stared at Mitch. "I'm assuming you're being rude like this because you want to make sure Lacey is safe around me."

"Possibly." Kasey closed his laptop. "And also because it does seem like you've been around when bad things happen. Plus, you studied at the same school Lacey did, which is definitely connected to this case."

Rosie slid out from the table. "I think I should go," she said quietly, looking at me. "Lacey, I'm still around if you need help with anything. That offer goes for all of you."

Giving Mitch and Kasey a dark look, I followed her outside, careful not to brush my nails against anything.

"Rosie, I don't know what their problem is. I don't think that stuff about you. You've been amazing, and I consider you a friend. I don't know what I would have done these last few days without you."

Rosie leaned a hip against the picnic table outside the trailer, shoving her hands in the pockets of her faded jeans. Tears glimmered in her eyes, and when she spoke, her husky voice held a slight tremor.

"I know you don't. And I understand why your friends are being like that. But it still hurts. All my life people have made assumptions about me because of how rough edged I am, and though it doesn't bother me much anymore, sometimes it still gets to me. It's partly why I finally left my job as a hairdresser and went back to the rodeo. Not near the same pay, but at least here, nobody looks down on you."

Kicking at a large piece of gravel with scuffed up boots that had patches of turquoise leather on the calf, she let out a heavy sigh.

"I ain't got nowhere to go for Christmas. Momma passed five years back, and Daddy's been gone since I was a kid. I don't got a family. And all my friends are busy with theirs. Yeah, they invite me over, but I would hate to intrude, and my boss at the fire station wouldn't let me work the holidays this year. He said I needed the time off."

"So you came to the rodeo and hoped to ride that high

through the new year, didn't you?" I remembered how busy my mother had worked to stay after Daddy had died. "Figured you'd camp here and start joining all the New Year's rodeos."

"Yeah. And when I found out you were in the same situation, I thought we could help each other get through it." Rosie's shoulders sagged. "But I don't think your friends would like that."

Reaching out, I touched the barrel racer's shoulder, certain my nails had set in the cold wind and wouldn't smudge.

"They'll live. Spend Christmas with us. Mitch and Kasey will behave, I promise. We don't have much in the way of food or comfort, but we'd love it if you joined us. No one should be alone on Christmas. I'll be at the hospital for most of it, but other than that, I'll be here."

After a long moment, Rosie hugged me. "I'll do that."

Turning, she walked to her trailer, sending me a wave before climbing the three stairs and shutting the door behind herself.

I sat down on the picnic table bench and rubbed my palms down the sides of my thighs, my jeans rough against my skin. The new nail polish glittered in the sunlight, and I studied it, remembering a time when my hands had looked just like Rosie's. Nails torn, palms covered in callouses from handling ropes and livestock. If I squinted, I could still see a scar on my left wrist from doing just that. Some days my hands itched to hold a bull rope again, and my ears yearned for the sound of a saddle creaking as I rode across the hills of Cody's ranch.

The squeak of the trailer door interrupted my reminiscing about the old days of rodeo life, and I looked up. Kasey crossed the small campsite, sneakers almost silent on the gray gravel. Brown hair tousled, the internet star settled his lanky frame next to mine, back pressed against the edge of the table. After a moment, he put an arm around my shoulder, and I leaned against him.

"We care about you, Lace," he said, and the use of my nickname made me smile even though I was still frustrated with his and Mitch's behavior.

"I know." I stared at his bright green shoes. "But you were so rude to Rosie, and she's been a rock for me. Barely knows me and has had my back this whole time."

"We can't afford to be careless," Kasey said. "Whoever is after you and Cody isn't going to stop until either you're dead or they're behind bars. We can't take a chance on anyone. No matter who they are."

"I'm scared this is life for me now." Taking a deep breath, I could taste old smoke from the campfire Rosie had burnt the night before.

"It won't be. I promise, and more than that, God won't let that happen."

"Is it just me," I shifted on the wooden bench, "or is everyone talking about God lately?"

Kasey stretched his legs out in front of us. "I'd say you're just noticing it now. God is everywhere, Lace. Even in our worst and most painful moments, He's with us."

"What about when we're being rude to people?" I asked, and Kasey let out a rueful chuckle.

"Even then. And yes, I will be apologizing to your friend. Not sure about Mitch."

After a minute, I stood and headed toward the trailer. "Let's start dinner," I said. "And go over the case again."

"We've gone over it a billion times." Kasey followed me.

Resting one foot on the bottom rung of the steps, I twisted to stare up at him. "And we're missing something. So let's go over it until we figure out what it is. Too many lives are at stake now, because if they're after me, they'll hurt you and Mitch to get to me."

"She sounds like a doll," Aubrey said into my ear later that night.

"A doll who likes to barrel race and put out fires," I chuckled, phone wedged between my shoulder and ear as I turned down the covers on my bed. Out in the living room, Kasey and Mitch were settling down for the night.

"And you said she's been in the bakery?" Aubrey's voice faded for a moment, and an object clanked in the background. The bakery owner never stopped messing around in the kitchen, and I wondered what sort of recipe she was coming up with now.

"A few times, yes. She raved about your food."

"I like her already," Aubrey laughed. "Describe her. I might remember her. Oh, and tell her next time she's in, it's on the house for being so nice to you."

"Well, she's about your height, blonde hair that's brown at the roots. Covered in tattoos and has more muscles than Blaze." I paused. "And she's got a really husky voice for a woman."

"Does she happen to have a palm tree tattoo by her ear?" Aubrey's voice grew distant for a moment before getting loud again.

"I—she does, actually," I said. "How did you know?"

"Does she also have a scar down her forearm that goes through a longhorn tattoo?" Aubrey's tone was serious.

"You're scaring me," I said. "Yes, she has that too. But how do you know?"

"Rosie came into the bakery not even a week ago. I remember her not so much because of how she looks or sounds but because of how inquisitive she was. Asked a lot of questions about Cody, and when I told her there wasn't much I can say out of respect for his privacy, she said she would be in the same rodeo as him."

"So maybe she had the times when she visited Flamingo Springs mixed up."

"Maybe," Aubrey agreed. "But Greg was in the diner at the time, getting breakfast on the sly since Blaze had told all the ranch hands not to leave the property, and they struck it up like old friends and even sat together."

The sudden shiver down my spine had me sitting on the edge of the bed hard even as my hands became clammy. "Aubrey, what are you saying?"

"I'm saying I thought she was an old friend passing through. And maybe that's all it was, and I'm being crazy. But don't you find it just a little bit odd someone killed Greg two days later, and Rosie has just happened to be around every time something has happened to you since you left Flamingo Springs?"

"I think you've just given me a lot to think about." I ran a hand through my hair, my inhale shaky.

"Could be nothing," Aubrey said. "But you need to be careful."

My answer was cut off when the lights in the bedroom went out.

"We just lost power. I'll call you tomorrow."

Ending the call, I fumbled my way to the door, muttering under my breath until I could figure out how to turn on my phone's flashlight app.

"Please tell me you have a battery backup," Mitch said from the couch, his flashlight almost blinding me.

"Yes," Kasey said from his spot on the bed the table folded into. "We L.A. boys can't handle this type of cold."

"Let's go outside and check the breaker box first," I said. "The trailer does have propane and a battery backup, but I'm not comfortable using the propane. Cody thinks the lines could be damaged from the fire the other night."

Shrugging into one of Cody's denim jackets, I took a deep breath as the scent of his aftershave surrounded me before slipping my boots on.

I leaned against the wall by the door while Mitch and Kasey struggled to get dressed in the near darkness, spots still dancing in front of my eyes from Mitch's flashlight.

"Ouch!" Mitch yelped, the trailer rocking back and forth as he fell. "My toe!"

"Well, it shouldn't have been in the way," Kasey said, and I fought to hide my snort of laughter.

Once the two were finally ready, we went outside to the electrical box where the trailer was plugged in. Checking the breaker on the side, I flipped it, but the trailer remained dark.

"Let's check a few other outlets," I said, walking into the next campsite and plugging in the phone charger I'd stuck in the pocket of Cody's jacket.

"Anything?" Kasey's teeth all but chattered as he stood next to me, hands jammed in his pockets. The sky above us was a black blanket sprinkled with glistening stars and a sharp breeze whipped across the campground.

I checked my phone.

"No," I said. "It's not charging. Let's try a few others." I glanced over at Rosie's trailer. Her truck was gone, and I wondered when she'd left, and where she'd gone. I had a few questions for my new friend, and we were going to start with why she'd lied to me.

Five campsites later, we admitted defeat.

"The whole campground must be out." I sighed.

"We're gonna freeze, aren't we?" Mitch muttered, and despite myself, I chuckled.

"No. The trailer has a battery backup. We can't charge our phones or anything, but it'll power the heat."

"What's the point of a backup if you can't use the lights?" Kasey held the door for me as I clambered into the trailer, almost tripping over someone's shoe.

"It's low on juice," I said. "Cody planned on getting a new

one after this trip. It wasn't a big deal because propane is his first choice if he's in a spot where there's no electricity."

Mitch checked his phone, once again blinding me. "I've only got thirty percent left."

"Mine's at twenty-eight," Kasey chimed in, and they both turned their flashlights off.

Staring down at my phone screen, my stomach tightened. "And I have fifteen. I was about to charge it when the power went out."

"Our charger blocks were charging," Mitch said, dismay evident in his voice. "They were completely dead because we accidentally left them in the car. They're how we power our Wi-Fi."

"It'll be all right." I moved past them to the small cabinet beneath Kasey's bed. "We'll go to the hospital tomorrow and charge everything. One night without the internet won't kill us."

Squatting down, I opened the small door and reached in, flipping the breaker that would switch the trailer to the battery. After a moment, the heat clicked on, the hum of the fridge a moment later, and we all let out a sigh of relief.

"There are flashlights and lanterns above the couch," I said. My phone let a chirp, warning me it only had nine percent battery left. After sending Aubrey a quick text letting her know what going was on, I forwarded it to Rosie so she wouldn't be taken off guard whenever she got back. A moment after, the screen went dark.

Mitch clicked on a lantern, turning it to dim and setting it on the kitchen counter. "At least we've got heat." He sighed. "We can figure the rest out tomorrow."

Taking the flashlight he offered, I made my way back to the bedroom and kicked my boots off. Still wrapped in Cody's jacket, I crawled into bed and pulled the blankets over my head.

Surrounded by Cody's scent, I closed my eyes, sending up a quiet prayer of thanks that the battery worked.

It wasn't long before I dozed off, the sounds of Mitch snoring in the living room as the heater rumbled a pleasant backdrop.

Peace filled the room, and I knew no matter what happened, everything would be all right.

10

The sound of chucks being kicked away from the trailer tires positioned below the bedroom woke me sometime later, and I squinted in the darkness. The trailer was silent, the air cool. The battery must have given out.

"Mitch, is that you?" I called out, sitting up in bed as boots crunched on the ground outside.

An engine roared to life as my feet hit the floor, and the trailer jerked forward, sending me flying face first into the wall.

"Ow!" I yelped as warm blood gushed from my nose. One hand pressed against my face, the other fumbled to open the door as I struggled to keep my balance, the trailer continuing to lurch forward.

"What in the world!" Kasey's exclamation was sleepy as I stumbled into the living room, blood dripping between my fingers and down my forearms. An abrupt turn had me falling on top of him, and he grunted as my elbow connected with his chest.

Sudden light filled the room as Mitch turned the lantern on, and we stared at each other. A coffee cup slid across the counter and fell to the floor where it bounced once before breaking in half.

"This isn't happening," Mitch said, and I could hear the panic in his voice. "We are *not* being kidnapped right now."

"Lacey, your face!" Kasey pushed me off him, his cheeks splattered with my blood.

"I hit the door with my nose." I tried to gain my balance.

Mitch made his way to the front door, testing the handle. "It's locked," he said, swaying back and forth, the lantern in his hand casting moving shadows around the room. He shoved on the door with his shoulder. "Whoever it is must've locked it from the outside."

"I'm the only one with the keys." I climbed on top of Kasey and jerked on the red emergency exit handle on the window.

"Let me," Kasey said, moving me out of the way. Grunting, he wrapped both hands around the handle, but it wouldn't budge, the window shades crumpling as he pressed against them.

"Try the one in the bedroom." I grabbed a dishtowel from the counter and held it to my nose. "Though I'm pretty sure I know what's gonna happen."

Standing, Kasey started toward the bedroom, holding onto the counter for balance. The trailer made a sharp right as it was pulled onto pavement, and the sudden movement sent Kasey flying headfirst into the bedroom while Mitch crashed into the door.

"God, we could use some help down here," Mitch groaned. "Because I think that lantern just busted my shin."

"Your shin," Kasey scoffed from the bedroom. "I'm pretty sure I just broke my wrist. For real." A loud grunt filled the air. "And this exit is blocked too. I thought emergency exits were tamper proof."

"We can't break the windows, either," Mitch said. "This is plexiglass. We'll never get through it."

"Everyone come get on the bed with me," I ordered. "This is the safest place in the trailer right now."

My nosebleed had slowed, but I could feel my eyes swelling. After removing the towel, I gingerly touched the bridge of my nose. When it moved to the side, I swallowed hard, determined not to throw up and make our situation any worse.

Mitch landed next to me, Kasey following a moment later, and upon inspection, confirmed he had indeed broken his wrist, and I'd broken my nose. The first aid kit Cody kept under the sink offered just enough bandages and painkillers to get Kasey situated, and the instant ice pack brought relief to my throbbing face.

Mitch's leg was banged up, but out of the three of us, he was in the best shape and did quick work bandaging Kasey's wrist before tending to my nose. The bandages on my burnt hand were soaked with blood, and he changed them, hands gentle as they grazed my blisters.

"Okay," he said, taking charge. "Our phones are dead. We're locked in the trailer. No one knows where we are now, and we won't be missed until sometime tomorrow night. I don't even know what time it is, so we could be on the other side of Texas before anyone figures out we're missing."

"Who cares about that?" Kasey leaned his head against the wall as he huddled under a blanket. "I wanna know who the maniac is who's kidnapping us!"

"I have an idea," I said quietly, the pavement beneath the trailer tires quiet.

"And?" Mitch pulled another blanket over himself even as I unbuttoned Cody's jacket, its sheep lining overheating me.

"It's Rosie. It has to be." I quickly filled my friends in on what Aubrey had told me. "I didn't think she was dangerous. Sometimes people lie because they're embarrassed about something, and I thought that's why she'd misled me."

"Well, maybe it's not her," Kasey said, but I shook my head, regretting my actions as my headache worsened with the movement.

"Who else would it be?"

"More than that, what are her plans for us?" Mitch's voice was so quiet I almost missed what he said.

We were silent for a long time after, and I leaned my head against the wall beneath the window. One hand tightly clutched Mitch's, the other grasping Kasey's while they both prayed, and I sent up a few prayers of my own.

"Just let me see Cody again, God," I whispered. "That's all I want. Just let me see him again."

"That was a right turn out of the campground," Kasey said a while later, still holding my hand.

"East," Mitch replied. "She's heading east. At least for now."

"Well, she'll have to stop for gas at some point," Kasey said hopefully. "And we can make enough noise to garner attention."

"Not for a very long time," I said. "Rosie's truck has a secondary gas tank. That must be where she was last night. Filling it up after cutting the power to the campground. That much gas, even with pulling this trailer, she'll be able to go a good six hundred miles before needing to stop."

"Well once it's light out, we can go to the windows and get the attention of other drivers," Mitch said confidently. "We're gonna get outta this, Lacey."

"I wanna believe that, I really do," I whispered. "But I already looked out the window when you guys were trying the emergency exits. They've been painted over. I tried shining a light out of one."

"My question is," Kasey grumbled, "how in the world we slept through all this. How did we not hear anything?"

"The heater was pretty loud," Mitch said consolingly. "And we're all exhausted."

"And now we've been kidnapped." I sighed. "Merry Christmas to us."

"And on that note," Mitch said. "How about we all try to sleep while we can? God only knows what's in store for us, and we need to be as ready as possible."

The soft snore to my left had me chuckling despite the dire circumstances.

"I think Kasey is already starting on that," I whispered. "Those painkillers don't take long."

"Good," Mitch whispered back. "I didn't want to say anything, but he's got a bad break, Lacey. It needs medical attention yesterday. It's not through the skin, but his hand is turning black—he's losing circulation."

"Mitch, I'm scared." Letting Kasey's hand go, I turned and buried my face in Mitch's shoulder even as my nose protested.

After a moment, my friend wrapped his arms around me. "I know. I am too. But now more than any other time in our lives, we gotta trust God. He's always with us, and I have a feeling He's gonna bring you back to Cody."

Hot tears burned my swollen eyes and stung my broken nose as they slipped down my cheeks and dampened Mitch's shirt.

"But how do you know God will be with us?" Shivers went through my body as fear threatened to strangle me.

"Because I have faith in God's word," Mitch told me. "He said He is with us always, and He's given His angels charge over us, to keep us in all our ways. I believe that with all my heart. Faith is moving forward and trusting the next step of the ladder will be there even if we don't see it."

Shifting, Mitch settled down, pulling me against him as Kasey snored away next to us.

"Go to sleep, Lace. Hard as it is, we've got to get rest."

The idea of sleep seemed impossible, but as Mitch began to

pray again, I found myself dozing off, and the last thing I heard was the promises of the Bible whispered over me.

"From what I can see out the vent, it's gotta be close to noon," Kasey said several hours later as he stood on the toilet and looked through the exhaust fan outside.

Sneakers squeaking as he turned and stepped down to the floor, he looked pale, holding his bruised wrist to his chest.

Pushing past him, I stepped onto the toilet lid, taking a deep breath of fresh air. Frowning, I took another deep inhale.

"What?" Kasey rested his uninjured hand on my leg to keep me steady.

I sniffed again. "I don't know, but the air smells different. Almost, swampy, if that makes sense."

"Say that again," Mitch called from the couch.

"Say what again?" I asked, stepping to the floor.

"You said it smells swampy," he said. "And none of us are wearing our jackets anymore because it's warm in here even though it's the end of December, and yesterday, we were freezing."

"East," I said slowly. "You guys said she turned east."

"Louisiana," Kasey said, almost falling into the shower when the trailer hit a bump. "She's heading into Louisiana."

"Well if she's gonna do what I think she's gonna do," Mitch said as Kasey and I sat back down on the bed next to him," we better figure out how we're gonna get out of this trailer, and fast."

"Like we haven't already?" Kasey's voice was filled with pain.

"The bayous." Mouth dry, I looked at Mitch through eyes that were now swollen slits. "No one will ever find us there."

"There's got to be a way out of this trailer," he said.

"We've tried everything," Kasey argued. "The door, the

windows, the exhaust vent, and the AC unit. Mitch, we're stuck."

"Nope," Mitch replied stubbornly. "We're not stuck. We're just at a red light."

"What do you have in mind?" I asked, seeing the frown that crossed his face.

"Doesn't this thing have outside storage that's accessible from inside?" he asked.

"Yeah, under the couch," I said. "But it locks from the outside."

"How strong of a lock though?" Mitch knelt in front of the couch and pulling on the panel beneath it.

After a moment, it gave way, and a crack of light shone from under the couch, coming from the edges of the outside storage door. Joining him, I laid on my stomach and crawled as far as I could under the couch while he shone a flashlight in front of me.

Various pieces of rodeo equipment dug into my ribs as I pushed at the small door, which would be big enough for us to wiggle through if we could get it open.

"It's locked," I grunted, struggling to breathe as something pressed into my stomach, almost gagging at the smell of oil and horse.

"Here." Mitch slid something to me. "Those locks aren't that strong."

I grabbed the screwdriver he'd found and wedged it against the metal hook keeping the door closed. Sweat dripped down my forehead, and I shoved hard as I could. The crack of light grew a bit bigger as the lock began to weaken, and after a moment, Mitch dragged me out from under the couch by my legs.

"My turn," he said. "I don't care what it takes, we're getting out of here."

We took turns for the next several minutes, prying at the

lock, the line of light steadily getting bigger until on my fourth turn, the lock gave way. Pushing the door up, I saw a blur of red-stained pavement, a tell-tale sign of clay found in the south.

"Kasey, let's go," Mitch called to our friend who was passed out on the bed.

"Mitch, we're on the interstate," I protested. "We jump out now, it'll kill us."

"Oh, right." He pulled me out from under the couch again.

"Soon as she slows down, we're going," I said. "So we've got to be ready."

The trailer slowed, and we stared at each other.

"We're still going too fast." Sweat dripped down Kasey's face. Fingers so swollen his knuckles had all but disappeared, he grimaced.

"She just left the interstate," Mitch said. "At some point, she's got to slow down enough for us to get out. Roads down here are awful."

"I hope so," Kasey said into his camera. He and Mitch had decided to film as much as possible in hopes that when we escaped, the footage would help the police.

The next few minutes seemed to drag on as the trailer jerked and lurched forward as it was pulled down pothole filled roads. Every time we thought it was safe to jump out, the truck would accelerate, and we'd find ourselves waiting again.

"The trees are over the road," Mitch called from his place in the bathroom as he looked out the small exhaust vent. "Kinda smells too."

"Cody and I spent a lot of time in Louisiana for rodeos." I sat on the edge of the bed. Picking up my bottle of water from where I'd wedged it between the couch cushions, I took a long sip. "These bayous and swamps stretch for miles. Even if we get out, we're gonna have a long walk ahead of us."

"I've got five bottles of water and our phones in the bag." Kasey gestured to his laptop bag. He looked back at the camera.

"As well as some flashlights and some food in case we get caught in the dark."

Swallowing another gulp of water, I glanced at him. "Let's hope not. There are too many predators down here to be caught in the dark."

We were silent after that, Kasey shutting the camera off as my words hung in the air. No matter what choice we made, our lives were at risk. Stay in the trailer and succumb to whatever Rosie had planned, or escape outside and brave the wild nature of the bayous.

Almost an hour later, the truck made a sharp left and slowed, and when the speed stayed the same, I glanced at my friends.

"Kasey, you go first," Mitch said. "Lacey, you're second."

"What if she sees us?" I asked. "What then?"

"Run," Mitch told me. "We're safer out there than we are in here."

"I hope you don't eat those words," Kasey mumbled as he shoved his legs under the couch. "Or rather, I hope a gator don't eat you."

"Oh, God," I whispered as I slung Kasey's bag over my shoulder. "Please let this work."

Giving us one last grim look, Kasey slithered the rest of the way under the couch and looked beneath it. His head disappeared as he dropped to the ground.

The trailer came to a sudden halt that sent me flying into Mitch, and he shoved me under the couch.

"We've been caught," he said. "Go!"

Sliding forward on my elbows, I went headfirst out the opening, turning as I did as if I was falling from the back of a bull. The movement had me landing on my shoulder on the red dirt road, and I rolled with it, the impact almost knocking the air from my lungs.

"She's got a gun—Lacey, run!"

I looked to my right. Rosie stepped out of the truck, a shotgun in her hand. Moss-covered trees towered over the road, their roots hidden by murky water. I glanced to my left and saw Kasey sprinting down the road.

"Kasey, get off the road!" I screamed, clambering to my feet and bolting forward off the edge of the road. Warm water oozed into the sneakers I'd changed into, and I prayed my feet would only come in contact with mud and not a gator.

"Lacey, get down!" Mitch's warning came just in time, and I fell on top of Kasey's bag as Rosie fired the gun. Pellets slammed into the tree above me, and I thought she'd missed completely until hot pain dotted my back.

"Let her go!" Mitch's voice was a roar.

I flipped over onto my tailbone, hands braced in the slimy mud. Mitch fell out of the storage door to the ground. Rosie turned the gun on him just as he lurched forward, his shoulder connecting with her knees. Mitch was no stranger to the gym, but neither was Rosie, and her training in barrel racing as well as being a first responder gave her the upper hand against the internet star.

"Lacey, get out of here!" Mitch struggled against Rosie as she slammed him into the side of the trailer.

"We can take her," I yelled at Kasey as I climbed back onto the road. Soaking wet, the thick smell of clay and decaying leaves filled my nose as mud slid down my arms.

The words had barely left my mouth when Rosie slammed Mitch's head into the trailer, her hand around his throat.

Mitch slid to the ground as Kasey jumped toward Rosie. They struggled over the shotgun, and his agonized scream filled the air when her boot connected with his broken wrist. Falling back, he raised his arms, trying to protect himself, his strong cross jab sending Rosie stumbling back.

Stepping back, he tripped over Mitch's limp body, and Rosie

was able to get the upper hand. Grabbing the shotgun, she brought the butt of it down on Kasey's temple, and he went still.

Turning toward the swamp, Rosie looked at me. "You can do this the easy way, or the hard way. Either you can come join your friends and die a peaceful death in the trailer, or you can let nature have you."

I took a step back, mud oozing between my toes as I clutched Kasey's bag to my chest.

"No matter what happens when we get out," Mitch had told me a few hours earlier, "I want you to run. If you gotta leave us behind, do it. Kasey and I are willing to die for you, Lace. No matter what, run. Someone has to stop her, no matter the price."

Rosie chuckled. "You sure are a stubborn thing." Turning, she leveled a kick at Mitch's ribs, and his groan filled the air. Looking back at me, she waggled her fingers. "I'm sure the gators will enjoy that about you."

Taking another step back, I put the tree between us, the sky almost hidden by the vines that crisscrossed between the trees. Another step led to another, and once I knew I was out range of the shotgun, I turned and ran, water sloshing around my calves.

The road quickly disappeared behind me, and I made a sharp left, hoping to be able to find it again once I'd put enough distance between Rosie and me.

Moss-covered trees stretched out in front of me. The sound of water gently slapping against them mixed with the chirping of the birds overhead. If I didn't know better, I'd have no reason to believe I was surrounded by predators.

I was in more danger than I'd ever been, and the only way out of it was straight through.

IT'S NOT EXACTLY easy to walk in a straight line in a bayou, and before long, I found myself turned around. The treetops had grown so close together I couldn't find the sun to know which direction I faced. Already dim, the murky light continued to grow fainter and fainter as evening came, and my legs burned from slogging through mud and climbing over logs and tree roots.

A deer carcass to my right had me gagging, and I wondered what had killed it. Panthers and gators were the top predators down here, but they weren't my only concern. Wild pigs, snakes, and spiders were also rampant, and when a large spider crawled down my arm when I brushed past a tree, the scream I let out startled the several birds nesting in it.

"I've got to get out of here before dark," I whispered to myself, shuddering. "If the wildlife doesn't get me, my heart is going to give out."

I looked at the sky again. The bits and pieces that were visible had softened to a dusky pink, and I knew time was short before it was completely dark.

Worry for Mitch and Kasey had my stomach in knots, and I prayed for them, not knowing if they were even alive. If I ever got out of here, I was going to do everything possible to find them.

Sweat trickled down my back, stinging the areas hit by the shotgun pellets. The bandage on my burnt hand was stained and soaked with bayou water, and I winced as I grabbed a tree branch, a blister breaking open. The thought of infection crossed my mind, and I did my best to ignore it.

Kasey's bag felt heavy on my shoulder as I tried to keep it from getting wet. All our phones were inside, along with Kasey's laptop and camera. As soon as I found help, I'd call Blaze and charge my phone so I could contact Mitch and Kasey's families.

Grime coated my arms, feeling rough against my skin when

I wiped my forehead, the humid air determined to suck every drop of moisture out of me. Hoisting the bag back up on my shoulder, I started forward again, panic trying to settle into my stomach. Somewhere several yards behind me, something made a loud splash, and I whimpered, knowing exactly what had caused it.

Despite my best efforts to stay by the road, I'd ventured deep into the bayou, and the water was now above my knees. The trees were more spaced out now, and I had a feeling the log floating about eight yards away was actually an alligator, though thankfully, a small one.

Moss tickled my face as I walked under a tree, and I yelped when something crawled across my neck. "The Lord is my Shepherd," I said under my breath, heart pounding in my ears as I took a gulp of air. "That means You protect us from wolves, right God? Well how about gators and panthers? Does Your rod and staff work on them too?"

A damp breeze lifted my blood crusted hair off my shoulders, and the creaking of a tree next to me had me whirling. Water slapped against my thighs as the ground beneath my feet sloped.

"Be still," a small voice said.

"Excuse me?" I asked. "Be still? Right now, in the middle of a swamp?"

"Be still," the voice said again. Gentle but firm, it brought me up short, brown water swirling between my legs, the laptop bag heavy as it pulled on my aching back.

The deep roar of a bull alligator filled the air, and I climbed up on the tree stump next to me that jutted a few feet above the water. Sneakers squeaking as I stood, I looked around, wondering how close I was to the large reptile.

"I'm not over there," the voice whispered again. I was transported back to Sunday school where a young teacher moved figures across a flannel board. Explaining that when

Elijah had fled to the mountain, he'd encountered God in the most unusual way and was never the same, the teacher's voice had been filled with awe as she read the Bible story. "Was God in the mighty wind that blew around the mountain?" the teacher asked as she moved a piece of blue flannel across the board.

"No," the class answered.

"What about the earthquake?" She added a piece of brown cloth.

"Not there either," I had yelled out, proud of having the right answer.

"And what about the fire? Was God there?" The teacher added one last piece to the board and turned to face us. "He wasn't, was He? Instead, God was the still, small voice that spoke to Elijah."

Hands clasped in front of her denim dress, the teacher's smile was gentle. "When everything seems crazy, and it seems like God is nowhere around, remember that in reality, He's so close that a little whisper is all that's needed for you to hear Him, if you open your ears."

"Open your ears," the voice whispered. I stared into the dark water below as a snake swam by. Taking a deep breath, I closed my eyes and attempted to quiet myself, my heart pounding so hard against my chest I thought for sure it would burst through my ripped shirt. Frowning, I squeezed my eyes tighter, mouth filled with the taste of swamp, broken nose stinging as damp air filled it.

"Okay, God. I'm opening my ears and trusting You. What now?"

A low rumble filled the air, and my eyes flew open. Stepping down from the stump, I turned in the direction the sound had come from. Barely breathing, I waited for the noise. When it came again, I stepped toward it. The road Rosie had taken us on had looked like a logging road, and I was certain the noise was from a logging truck. Walking as fast as I could, I made my way toward the rumble, stumbling multiple times in the near darkness but unwilling to tie up my hands with the flashlight Mitch had packed in the bag.

The sky was almost pitch black by the time I reached the road, and only then did I get the flashlight out. I still wasn't out of danger, as panthers and gators preyed along the roads, but I could finally breathe a sigh of relief.

"I just need another trucker to come along, Lord," I whispered as I walked down the middle of the red road, my wet shoes covered in clay.

A possum ran in front of me, baring its sharp teeth as the flashlight shone into its beady black eyes, and I stepped back, knowing how vicious the little creatures could be. Above me, a bat screeched. The sky occasionally flickered with lightening, and I shivered when a drop of rain landed on my head.

The shaking ground alerted me a truck was coming long before its headlights were visible. Coming to a stop, I jumped up and down, shining my flashlight at the windshield as more drops of rain landed on my sweat-soaked head.

Grinding to a halt, the large logging truck filled the road. The vehicle's headlights almost blinded me as the driver's door opened, and a man climbed out of the cab.

"You alright, love?" he asked, stepping toward me.

"Can you call the police?" I asked, tears running down my face, legs giving way.

He caught me as I went down, muttering in French when he caught sight of my bruised face.

"God have mercy," he said in English as he half carried me to his truck. Pushing me up into the cab, he grabbed his phone from the middle console and dialed the emergency number before climbing behind the seats into his sleeping area.

"I have no signal," he said. "Let me turn my Wi-Fi on."

Moving to the back of the cab, he fiddled with something by his bed before trying his phone again.

"Yes, my name is Jack, and I just picked up a woman on Logging Road 42. I'm taking her to the hospital in Many, but we need a police officer to meet us there. She is very hurt."

Climbing back into the front of the cab, he opened the first aid kit he'd grabbed from beneath the back of his seat.

"*Chérie*, what is your name?" he asked. The dispatcher said something on the other end of the line as Jack pushed me down into the passenger seat.

"Lacey Baker," I whispered, tears running down my bruised face as a small dog jumped into my lap.

"Darcy," Jack scolded the dog before repeating my name to the dispatcher. "She's a missing person, you say? Well, she is with me, and she's in rough shape. Yes, I'll keep my phone on me. Yes, sir."

Ending the call a few moments later after giving the dispatcher as much information as he could, Jack grabbed Darcy from my lap and placed her on his.

"Here." He handed me a bottle of sports drink and a sandwich from a small cooler behind my seat. "Eat this and then take the painkillers from the kit." He leaned over and dabbed at a cut on my cheek, the smell of antiseptic strong in my swollen nose.

"Your back needs attention." He pulled away even as Darcy leaned forward from her owner's lap and took a gentle nibble of my sandwich. "Anywhere you've bled, we need to put medicine on it. The swamp is full of fungus, and staph infection is easy to get down here."

Squeezing the sandwich, I stared at Jack. Could I trust him? Eyes narrowed, he watched me, Darcy leaning forward for another nibble.

"All right." I turned my back to the truck driver so that he could tend my wounds through the several holes in my shirt, unwilling to pull it up.

"This will hurt," Jack said, and the sound of a bottle being opened reached my ears. "This will do for the time being, but you need to see a doctor sooner than later. There are definitely some pellets lodged in your back."

His somber words were the only warning I had before he pressed an alcohol-soaked cotton pad to my back. The cry I let out echoed through the truck, and I clenched the sandwich, the bread falling apart on my lap, crumbs dusting the laptop bag between my feet.

"Just a few more minutes," Jack whispered, hands gentle as he tended to my wounds. "Some of them need bandages. Darcy, move."

The metal lid of the first aid kit clanged shut, and after a brief pause, Jack pressed a bandage onto my lower back, then two more by my left shoulder blade.

"Here." Crawling into the back of the cab again, he handed me a shirt. "Put this on."

Biting my lip as my sore body cried out, I slowly slipped into the clean one Jack gave me, pulling it over my mud-stained clothes. Soft against my skin, the shirt smelled of motor oil and tobacco. "I'm taking you to the hospital."

"You can't!" I turned to face the blond truck driver. "The person who did this to me still has my friends. They could be dead by now—we have to find them!"

Jack leaned back for a moment and studied me.

"How long were you in the swamp?" He wadded up the blood-soaked cotton ball and shoved it into a plastic bag at his feet. Grabbing the bottle on his dash, he scrubbed his hands with sanitizer.

"Most of the day." I quickly changed the bandage on my hand and wrapped it in clean gauze after spreading ointment on it. "But besides my broken nose, I'm okay. I just need some food and water. We have to find my friends. They sacrificed themselves so I could get away."

Jack looked out the windshield at the road illuminated by his headlights. "I prayed this morning. God, surely there is more to life than transporting logs, and here you are." He shook his head. "*Chérie*, as long as you're sure you're okay, let's go get your friends." Unlocking his phone, he handed it to me. "Call the police, eh? Tell them our plans."

Settling back in his seat, he put the truck in gear and hit the gas as I dialed the emergency number.

Explaining everything to the dispatcher, I asked if I could be patched through to the Flamingo Spring's police department. After eight rings, the call went to Blaze's cell phone, and he answered on the second ring.

"Blaze?" I sobbed.

"Oh, my word. Lacey!" he exclaimed. "Aubrey, it's Lacey!"

Quickly explaining everything, I asked him to call my mother before hanging up so he could get in contact with the other departments.

"There's not much they can do tonight, you know." Jack glanced at me as we rounded a gentle corner. Darcy was now sound asleep in my lap, her golden coat shimmering in the dim lights of the dash. "It's too dangerous to be out in the swamps at night, but soon as it's light, they'll be out there, and I'll be with them."

"I don't even know why she's doing this," I told my new friend, relaying the case to him as fast as I could. "All I know is she'll stop at nothing to silence everyone involved."

"I've driven this road many times," Jack said, his blond hair a halo around his head. "There aren't many turn-offs, but I know where they are, and we'll stop at each one. Why don't you rest until we reach one, yes? Darcy gives good snuggles."

Against my better judgement, I agreed, finishing the crushed sandwich I still held. Before long, I found myself dozing off as Darcy snored in my lap, her paws occasionally twitching.

Jack had an extra cable, and my phone sat on the dash as it charged, the screen occasionally lighting up as friends texted me. News of my rescue spread, and almost everyone in Flamingo Springs reached out. Too tired to reply, I only answered Blaze and Aubrey's texts, both working hard to reach Mitch and Kasey's families.

Jack woke me at every turn-off, and we got out and looked for tire tracks at each one, only to be disappointed every time.

"This is good, though," he said after the third one. "It means she hasn't carried her plan out yet as she's still looking for a place." The next turnoff isn't for almost an hour, and by then, it'll be light. Anything beyond that will have to wait, as logging trucks don't fit past that point."

I looked at my new friend, eyes filling with tears again. "What if they're dead, Jack?"

The Cajun truck driver let out a heavy sigh. "I don't have an answer for that, love. But we're going to find them. Let's not think past the next step, okay?"

Reaching across the console, he patted Darcy on the head before grasping my hand. "God got you out of that swamp and put me in your path. If He did that, He's with your friends."

Staring out the windshield, I took a deep breath as the first bits of sunrise began to streak across the sky. Tears leaked from the corners of my eyes as I focused on the bits of gold light, clinging to the faith Jack offered me.

The night was almost over.

11

"Got a BOLO out for Rosie," a police officer said a few hours later. "And we're getting drones up in the sky so we have a map of what we're going into."

The sun now fully in the sky, dozens of police officers and search and rescue volunteers milled around the orange roadblock signs that stopped truckers from going any further. The road beyond the signs was narrow, the land barely touched, and fresh tire tracks led us to believe Rosie had been there.

"We've got camper tracks going in," an officer called over to us, "but not coming out. She was definitely here."

The wind creaked in the trees above us, and despite the fact Christmas was just around the corner, sweat trickled down my back in the humid Louisiana heat. The police had brought me a change of clothes, and the new sneakers I wore were already covered in red dust from the clay road.

I'd managed to pull my tangled, dirty hair into a ponytail and carefully wash my face with a baby wipe. From the concerned looks everyone gave me, I still looked as terrible as I felt.

Taking a sip of hot chocolate from the thermos someone had handed me, I stared past the roadblocks. Treetops overgrown by vines and moss made visibility limited, and the cops handed out reflective vests. A few search and rescue members had chest waders folded and strapped to their backs. Except for myself and one other person, everyone had a gun on their hip.

"Considering how wet that camera was, the memory stick works great," an officer told me, her red hair bright beneath her cap. Blue eyes twinkling, she pecked at the laptop she'd set up on the hood of a squad car. Something about her reminded me of Misty, and I was overwhelmed with homesickness for my friends.

"We've got aerial footage," someone said a moment later. "Let's head out. I need everyone to remember you have got to watch every step. Thing about the bayou is pretty much everything can kill you. Stick to the buddy system and keep your eyes open."

Jack fell in step with me as we followed the group, several of the officers muttering into the radios strapped to their chests. A member of the local news outlet trudged behind us, the man next to her talking quietly into the camera she fixed on him. The case had sparked national attention, and I'd left my phone in Jack's truck, nauseated from the online article I'd read about myself as it detailed the abuse I'd endured.

"We're gonna find them," Jack said. "I've got a good feeling about it." He'd left Darcy in the cab with a bowl of kibble, and after a moment of walking, he reached out and grabbed my hand.

"Your cowboy sure is a lucky man," he told me.

"I'm the lucky one." I squeezed his warm hand. "And I can't wait for the next few weeks to be over with."

"Guys, we've got eyes on the trailer," the officer in charge said, touching his earpiece. "About two miles ahead." He tapped his ear again. "What's the ETA for that rescue truck, Rebecca? This is rough country to try to backpack two people out on foot."

After a brief pause, he mumbled something and picked up the pace. I struggled to keep up, my side aching from when I'd fallen from the trailer the day before.

The road dwindled down until the tracks from the truck and trailer dipped into the water on either side, and I wondered how Rosie had been able to get out. The sounds of wildlife were loud, and I struggled not to sneeze, clay dust filling my throbbing nose.

"There it is!" Jack pointed in front of us, and I looked up from watching where I stepped. The tail end of the camper stuck out of the swamp. Completely on its side with the storage cabinet we'd escaped from in the mud, its black exterior was rust colored with clay and dirt.

"Mitch! Kasey!" I yelled, pulling away from Jack and running forward. Jumping off the road, I stood knee deep in sludge, and a rescue member yelled at me about snakes. Ignoring them, I sloshed forward until I reached the trailer, digging in my pocket for Cody's keys, which I somehow hadn't lost. Something skittered away from me and under a tree root, the water rippling around it, but at this point, I couldn't care less what it was. All that mattered was getting to my friends.

"I need a boost," I said as the men with waders followed me. Jack reached me first, and bending, he made a stirrup with his hands for me to step on. Standing on the edge of the bank, the news crew member filmed us.

"One, two, three," he grunted, shoving upward, and my wet fingers squeaked across the metal of the side of the trailer as I scrambled to get on top. The dust made the metal slippery, and it took a few tries before I could climb up. Sliding to the door, I tried to put the key in the lock and let out a cry of dismay. "She's filled it in with glue!"

"Move out of the way." Jack climbed up next to me. Bending down, he grabbed the foldable machete an officer held up to him. Bracing his legs as water dripped from his green waders, Jack raised the machete above his head and brought it down on the lock. Sparks flew as metal connected with metal, and a few blows later, the entire handle broke off. Handing the machete to me, Jack knelt and wrestled the door open after shedding his waders.

"Hold it," he ordered me, and leaning over the opening, I held the door as he jumped down. Taking a deep breath, I shoved the door as hard as I could until the hinges bent, and it lay flat against the camper's side. After passing the machete to an officer about to join me, I hovered over the doorway.

Below me, Jack let out a whoop. "They're in here!"

A groan reached my ears as the trailer rocked beneath me, Jack moving around and muttering something in French.

"Mitch!" I yelled down. "Kasey!"

"Lacey?" Kasey weakly called out.

"I'm here. Is Mitch okay?"

"I don't know." Kasey's voice trailed off, and he let out another groan.

"Mitch is unconscious." Jack's voice drifted up to me as the officer next to me carefully lowered himself into the trailer. "He's lost a lot of blood, *chérie.*"

"I'm coming down," a young man who had just climbed up next to me said. The patch on his dark blue shirt said EMT, and sweat dripped down his tan cheeks as he handed a medical bag down to Jack.

The moments crawled by as he assessed Mitch and Kasey, Jack updating me on what Kasey told him.

"Nate?" the EMT called up to the head of the rescue group sitting next to me.

"Yeah, Zac?" Nate said, black curls shiny in the early morning light, dark skin glistening with sweat.

"Can they land a chopper anywhere near here? We need to airlift one of them to Shreveport."

"Rebecca," Nate spoke into his radio. "I need that truck now! And we need some air assistance. These guys are seriously injured. Where's the nearest one can land?"

"Give me a sec, and I'll let you know," Rebecca replied a moment later. "The truck will be to you in about ten minutes."

"We gotta get Mitch out of here," Jack yelled just as the smell of blood reached my nose.

"God help us," Nate muttered. "I don't know how we're gonna do that." He squinted at me. "I need you to get back on the ground and give us some space. If your friend is as messed up as Zac is saying, we're gonna have a problem getting him out safely."

Nodding, I turned and slid down the side of the trailer, my arm rubbing against a tire. Wincing as it tore the skin off my muddy forearm, I pressed a hand to the bloodied area as I made my way through the dirty water.

The rumble of the truck arriving a moment later almost drowned out the sound of mud sucking at my legs as I struggled to the shore. A shiver went through me as a sizable spider scurried across the bank in front of me.

A search and rescue member grabbed my hand, helping me up and onto firm ground, his grip warm. Shoving away the camera that had been pushed into my face, he led me back toward the road.

"Sit here." He pushed me onto a portable chair. "And eat this." He pressed a protein bar into my hands before making his way back to the trailer and clambering up onto it as the truck driver followed, carrying a folded-up stretcher.

The next hour was a blur as rescue members pulled Mitch and Kasey from the trailer. EMTs strapped Mitch to the stretcher, his neck in a brace to avoid jostling him.

Kasey could climb out on his own but collapsed on the side of the trailer and had to be carried.

"Chopper is about five minutes out," Rebecca said. "Seven miles south in a field."

"We're on our way," Nate responded a moment later. "Just let us get these boys situated."

"Lacey." Jack pulled me to my feet, the smell of swamp and sweat strong on him. "There isn't enough room in the ambulance or chopper for you to go with them. You can either ride with one of the officers or with me and Darcy. It's gonna be about a three-hour drive to Shreveport."

"With you," I whispered, leaning into the hug he offered.

"Good deal." He squeezed me tight, the scent of his soap momentarily overpowering the swamp smell. "Let's head out."

The walk back to the vehicles took forever, the ambulance now long gone. My shoes sloshed with every step I took, mud and clay oozing from them. Neck itching from the bite of some sort of insect, I scratched at it, every muscle in my body aching from the last few days.

Darcy covered my face in kisses as I climbed into the truck cab, wincing as I got mud all over the seat. Jack only shrugged, his own clothes soaked.

"Mitch looked so bad," I said as he stuck the key in the ignition. He'd detached the trailer of logs that morning and had no problem turning the cab around and heading down the road that would eventually lead to a highway.

"Once they get some fluids in him, he'll be okay," he assured me, but I'd heard the EMT when he'd said Mitch's chances weren't good, and I said as much.

"Gonna have to trust God. I know that's hard, but right now, that's the only option."

I glanced at the Cajun angel as he shifted gears, Darcy turning a few circles in my lap before settling down, her warm head resting on my uninjured forearm. "I know," I whispered after a long pause. "I know."

THE DRIVE to Shreveport felt both long and short, and my stomach tightened as Jack pulled into the hospital parking lot.

Just past noon, people in scrubs of various colors walked past us as we entered the foyer. We'd stopped halfway to get new clothes at a gas station, and I felt like a mess in my oversized sweatpants, LSU T-shirt, and tangled, blood-matted hair. Flipflops loud on the tile floor that had seen better days, I followed Jack across the cheerfully decorated waiting room.

"Can I help you?" a redheaded receptionist asked as we approached the desk, her southern drawl so thick I struggled to understand her.

"Yes, ma'am." Jack gave her an appreciative look. "We've got two friends who were airlifted here not too long ago.

"Names?" She barely glanced at Jack as she pecked at her keyboard, curly ponytail bobbing with her motions.

I stepped forward at Jack's gesture and gave her Mitch and Kasey's last names. After a moment, she looked up. "Mitch is still in surgery, but Kasey has been moved to a room on the third floor. He's in very rough shape but will be allowed visitors this afternoon once he's awake. The doctors put a few pins in his wrist so he'll be asleep for the next several hours." She squinted at me through her green-rimmed glasses, brown eyes concerned.

"Honey, I think you need to see a doctor yourself." She rolled her chair back as I swayed forward.

Placing my forearms on the counter, I swallowed hard, bile filling my mouth.

"Lacey?" Jack placed a warm hand on my back as I rested my head on my arms.

"I don't feel so good," I whispered, sweat breaking out on my upper lip.

"I need a nurse out here," the receptionist yelled as my knees gave out.

Jack grabbed me before I hit the floor, and the sound of someone running down the hall was the last thing I heard before everything went dark.

"I FIND THIS A LITTLE EXCESSIVE," I complained a few hours later to Jack after taking a sip from a large cup. The plastic straw felt rough against my chapped lips, but the icy water was refreshing to my dry throat.

"Nah," Jack countered from his spot in the chair next to my bed. "You threw up. A lot."

"Don't remind me." I set the cup down on the tray next to me. The AC unit outside my window hummed loudly, and I focused on the noise for a long moment, letting it soothe my headache.

"When you're ready, Kasey is awake and wants to see you," my nurse, Cassie, said as she hung my chart on the wall. "Your vitals are good, and the doctor got all the pellets out of your back with no issues. He just wants a full IV in you before he signs the release form, and you'll need to be in a wheelchair when you visit your friends."

After she left, I glanced at my phone, the bottom part of my vision blocked by the white gauze taped over my nose, which had finally been set. Dozens of missed calls and unread text messages filled the screen. I put it back down, not ready to answer everyone.

Brey was on her way from Flamingo Springs, the young waitress almost hysterical even though I'd told her Kasey would be okay.

"Do you think they'll catch Rosie?" I asked Jack as he dozed in the uncomfortable-looking chair. The smell of antiseptic filled the room, and I longed for a hot shower. The hospital gown I wore scratched against my skin.

Jack snorted. His mouth had fallen open as he'd drifted off. "I think so." He yawned. "Unless she had a different car she switched to, that rig of hers will be easy to spot, and she can't have gone far."

"I just wish I knew why."

The rest of my words were cut off by the buzz of my phone, and I picked it back up. The sight of Cody's name made my heart skip a beat, and I pressed the green icon to answer the call.

"Lacey?" Sounding weak, Cody's raspy voice filled my ear.

"I'm here," I whispered, throat tight as tears stung my eyes.

"Are you okay? You're all over the news."

"Am I okay?" I tried to laugh but ended up sobbing. "You're the one who's been in a coma."

"Lace." Cody's voice dropped. "Sweetheart, tell me you're okay."

"I'm alive, and right now that's enough."

Jack stood and stretched before disappearing into the restroom.

"Soon as they let me up, I'm on my way to you," Cody said. "We've wasted enough time."

"I agree." I leaned back against my pillows and fiddled with the rough material of the thin blanket that covered my legs.

"I love you, Lacey," Cody said so quietly I almost didn't hear him. "And I'm so sorry for what I've put you through."

Settling into the pillows, I wiped my eyes as we continued talking, and it wasn't until Cody fell asleep an hour later that I ended the call.

"Lucky man." Jack echoed his words from earlier.

"I'm just ready to go home and marry him." I chuckled

weakly as Cassie came in and removed the IV line from my arm. Except for the gauze on my nose and a few bandages on my arm from the time in the bayou, I was almost good as new.

"Well, until then, do you feel up to a shower and some clean clothes I rustled up for you?" she asked, hand on her hip. "It's no substitute for a wedding, but as much as you've been through, I bet it'll feel pretty close." Digging in the pocket of her cartoon-covered scrubs, she pulled out a small perfume vial. "I even have some peppermint body spray for you, if you'd like."

"I would love that. And then can I see my friends?"

"We'll see." She helped me stand and kept one arm around my waist as she guided me to the restroom.

Thirty minutes later, she helped me back to the bed where I sat, legs trembling.

Thanking her, I ran a disposable comb through my hair, loving the squeaky-clean feeling it had. For the first time in two days, I didn't smell like mud and sweat, and I smiled. The sweats Cassie had found were a size too big but were comfortable, and the charcoal gray made my yellow hospital socks stand out.

Cassie came back with a wheelchair a moment later and another stack of clothes she handed Jack.

"You shower," she told him. "And I'll take her to see her friends. Rooms 212 and 314, which is in the ICU."

Moments later, she wheeled me into Kasey's room, and I almost fell on my face as I stood and leaned over to hug him.

Face covered in bruises, his broken wrist was in a cast, and wires protruded from him. Brown hair slightly damp, his grin was weak but bright as he tried to hug me back.

"We made it," he whispered. "I told you we would."

"Brey's on her way," I told him, pulling back and falling into the wheelchair, which Cassie had thankfully set the brake on.

She left the room a moment later, and I bit my lip as I took in my friend's rough condition.

"Cody is awake," I said.

Nodding, Kasey's chestnut brown eyes squinted in pain at the movement, the vein in his forehead pulsing. "And Mitch?"

"Not yet. The nurse told me he has a severe head injury and some swelling on his brain. Rosie beat him up pretty bad."

"But we're alive." Kasey sighed. "That's what matters."

"I just want to know why she did this." I held his good hand in mine. Both were covered in scratches and bruises from the last few days.

"Definitely connected to Greg, but she didn't say anything to us except that no one would find us. Boy, was she wrong, because Lacey Baker doesn't back down."

I chuckled. "I had some help."

We talked a little while longer, and then I made my way to Mitch's room. The YouTuber was barely visible amid all the wires and gauze that surrounded him, and his eyes were almost swollen shut.

Multiple monitors beeped, and the sight of the breathing tube in his mouth had me squeezing my eyes shut. Rosie had clearly taken her anger from losing me out on him, and after a moment, I wheeled my chair closer to his bed and carefully rested a hand on his foot.

"God," I whispered. "Please take care of him."

"He will, *chérie*," Jack said, coming up behind me. "He's brought y'all this far. He won't leave you now."

"I want to go home, but I don't want to leave them," I said.

"Will you settle for getting out of here and into a hotel?" Jack grabbed the handles on the back of my chair and pushed me into the hallway.

"Once Brey is here, I would love that." Running a hand through my drying hair, I winced when I touched a bump from one of my falls in the trailer.

Leaning my head back, I stared at Jack.

"Why are you doing this? Acting like a best friend when we've only known each other for a day."

Jack smiled and touched the end of my nose with the tip of his finger. "When God tells you to do something, you listen. Learned that a long time ago."

"That's pretty cool that you listen to Him when there's other stuff you could be doing."

"What's He telling you, Lacey?" Jack asked, and I stared down the pale-yellow hallway before we entered my room. "What's He asking you to do right now?"

"To trust Him," I said after a long pause. Jack holding my arm, I climbed back onto my bed. "And that everything is going to work out."

My phone rang, cutting Jack's next words off, and I picked it up. "Hey, Blaze."

"They got her, Lacey," Flamingo Springs' sheriff said into my ear. "Caught her about half an hour ago."

Hands shaking so much I almost dropped my phone, I stared at Jack as he sat on the bed next to me.

"So it's over?" My voice trembled.

"Not quite." Paper rustled in the background. "She's got an accomplice. Whoever set fire to Cody's trailer is still out there."

"Oh. Right." The peace that had filled me quickly drained back out.

"It's almost over, though. I promise. We spoke for a few more moments, and after I ended the call, I looked up at Jack. "They got her."

"That was fast. I figured it'd be days before they caught her."

"There's still someone out there who worked with her, and that terrifies me."

"Lacey?" Brey ran into my room and flung herself at me, knocking me back onto my pillows.

"Tell me he's okay," she sobbed into my shoulder as I held her tight. Smelling of maple syrup and bacon, Kasey's girlfriend still wore her apron from Aubrey's diner.

"He is," I told her. "He's been awake and cracking jokes. Can't wait to see you, either."

Pulling back, Brey swiped a hand across her nose, face streaked with mascara.

"Thank God." More tears streamed down her cheeks and dripped onto my arms.

"Go see him. I'm getting a hotel room, and I want you to stay with me, if you'd like." I gave her a tight hug before sending her to Kasey's room, promising to text her the name of the hotel.

"It's almost seven." Jack checked his phone. "Let's get outta here and get some rooms at the place down the road, and then I'll go pick up supper for everyone. I think visiting hours are over at nine."

Four hours later, I settled into my bed at the nearby hotel, Brey already asleep on the couch by the window.

The hospital would release Kasey within the next few days, and the doctors were hopeful Mitch would pull through, though he'd have a long road of therapy in front of him. Cody's recovery journey was going well, and his parents were working to have him transported to a hospital closer to Flamingo Springs.

With Rosie in custody, it would only be a matter of time until the police caught her accomplice. Maybe then we'd be able to put everything behind us and move on.

Jack was next door with Darcy, and I breathed a sigh of relief, knowing the God-sent trucker would keep Brey and me safe. Turning on my side, it wasn't long before the last few days caught up with me, and I slipped into a deep sleep.

The night was finally over.

"Mitch is awake." Brey's voice was quiet when I answered her early morning call almost a week later.

"Thank God," I whispered, voice choked. "What are the doctors saying?"

"Too soon to know anything for sure, but they think he's going to be just fine."

Sitting on my small couch, I took a sip of coffee and stared blankly at the TV in front of me, the morning news host going on about some global crisis.

It'd been two days since I'd come home, and yesterday, Blaze had allowed me back into my apartment. The salon was still taped off, but I had no plans to reopen it until it was completely remodeled.

Brey had remained in Shreveport with the boys, everyone in Flamingo Springs taking turns to go stay with her. Cody stayed in a hospital an hour away, and life slowly resembled what it had once been.

Or so I kept telling myself.

Rosie's accomplice was still out there, and she'd refused to say a word to the authorities. Though it was unlikely anything else would happen, I still found myself on edge. Blaze's assurance that Rosie's friend would be caught did little to soothe me, and I said as much.

"How am I supposed to continue on with life knowing there's still someone out there who tried to kill me?" Setting my fork down, I stared at Blaze across the table in Aubrey's small kitchen, the bowl of chicken stew in front of me turning my stomach.

"One day at a time," Blaze replied evenly, dabbing the mustache he'd started growing with a paper napkin. "And one prayer at a time."

Aubrey touched my hand as it clenched my fork, careful to avoid the many scratches that still covered it from my ordeal in the bayou.

"You're not alone, Lacey," she said. "We're with you every step of the way, no matter if those are steps taken forward or backward."

Shaking myself, I came back to the present and scowled at my blurry reflection that stared up at me from my coffee cup. Blonde hair stood out from my head every which way, and my fingernails were chipped and uneven, my skin dry and chapped. Standing, I poured the coffee down the drain and rinsed the cup. "Come on, Lace," I muttered. "Time to get in the chute and show the bull who's boss."

Turning the TV off and some gospel music on, I set to cleaning my apartment, starting with the baseboards and working my way up. Blaze had already gone through Sarah's things and taken what he felt was necessary for the case, and the rest I boxed up, only keeping a few necklaces to remember her by.

The small Christmas tree in the corner twinkled with colored lights, and I straightened the silver star Sarah had placed on top. Holiday decorations were here and there, garland strung above the windows, and the gloom that had filled the apartment began to lift as I moved around.

By noon, I put the vacuum cleaner back in the hall closet. Two hours later, I emerged from the bathroom with a fresh manicure, neatly curled hair, and a face full of makeup.

Turning my laptop on, I spent the remainder of the day emailing clients and working with my insurance company to have the salon remodeled. Before I knew it, dinnertime had come and gone.

Snatching my keys, I headed a few towns over to the hospital Cody was rehabbing in, grabbing food along the way from a drive-thru.

"If I stay busy enough," I mumbled to myself as I crossed the parking lot, "maybe I'll be able to start moving forward." I let out a heavy sigh as I tossed my drive-thru trash into the garbage can by the sliding door. If only it were that easy.

Because Cody had been moved to a regular care room, visiting hours were until ten. After checking in at the front desk, as only Cody's parents, Blaze, myself, and a few others were allowed to see him, I jabbed the fourth-floor button on the elevator and stared at the floor as the door slid shut.

It'd been over two weeks since I'd seen Cody. Though we talked every night on the phone, butterflies still fluttered around in my stomach at the thought of getting to hug him.

The door to his room was open, and after knocking, I stepped in, surprised to see Mason sitting next to Cody's bed. Bald head bent, he stared at the chessboard set up on the table between him and his boss.

"Oh, I'm sorry," I apologized when they both looked up, startled. "I can come back—"

"Lacey!" Cody's excited exclamation cut me off as he opened his arms. After a moment's hesitation, I set my purse down on the counter by the door and crossed the room to his bed.

Strong arms wrapped around my waist as Cody almost pulled me off my feet, and I shyly hugged him back. Unable to hold back my sigh, I buried my face in his neck.

"I'm gonna go grab some snacks," Mason said, and a moment later, it was just my ex and me in the quiet room, the TV in the corner on mute.

"I've missed you," Cody whispered, finally letting me go. His hand was still wrapped in gauze, but his scratches and bruises had healed. Moving to the side, he pulled me down onto the bed next to him.

"How are the boys?" he asked as we stared into each other's eyes. "Mitch still improving?"

"Yes." I became acutely aware of the way our bodies were pressed together. "The hospital released Kasey this morning, and if Mitch stays on track, they'll let him go home next week. He'll need a lot of physical therapy to relearn some of his motor skills, but everything looks promising."

Putting his arm around my shoulder, Cody squeezed it before letting me go, blue eyes bright. "We made it through, Lace. Been quite a ride the last few weeks, but we made it through."

"Not exactly." I sighed, eyes tracing his face, noting that the color had finally come back into his cheeks. The fluorescent lighting caused the pink scar by his eyebrow to stand out, and I gently touched it.

"Because there's still one person left." He finished my thought, and I nodded, lowering my hand and fiddling with the edge of his pillow. The plastic side of the bed dug into my hip, and I shifted, looking at everything except the man next to me.

"Three people were murdered, Cody. And four more almost lost their lives. Except for Sarah and Dalton, we don't even know why."

"Rosie will end up talking," he reassured me as he rubbed my arm.

Looking back at him, I bit my lip. "I'm trying to believe that. I really am."

We were silent afterward, the scent of Cody's aftershave and the hospital smell whirling around us as the vent above his bed blew out lukewarm air, stirring my curls.

"Never suspected Greg of anything bad." Cody picked up a chess piece from his abandoned game with Mason and turned it over in his hands. "It's still hard for me to accept he murdered two people."

He studied the chess piece.

"Greg and I never got along from the moment you hired him," I said. "But I would never have suspected him of doing something so terrible."

"And with Tyler being in on some of it, even though he didn't know the full story, he's looking at a long time in prison." Cody sighed. "Lost my foreman and my assistant foreman just like that. And more than that, they were my friends."

"What about Mason?" I took the chess piece from Cody and placed it back on the board, its black finish gleaming in the light. "He's a good ranch hand and knows more about animals than anyone else I know. Teach him the business side, and he'd be great at it."

"I would, wouldn't I?" Mason interrupted as he strode back into the room, hands full of snacks from the vending machine down the hall.

Cody rolled his eyes. "I've been thinking about it."

"Think about this instead." Mason passed out snacks. Sitting back down, he moved a figure on the board. "Checkmate."

"Now how in the world?" Cody put his bag of chips down.

Chuckling, I leaned over his legs and tapped a spot on the board. "Not checkmate. He's still got one more move."

Both men stared at the board for a long moment before nodding.

"She's right," Mason said.

"Of course I am." I smirked. "Cody and I played chess almost every night when we were on the road back when I was still in the rodeo. He's yet to win a round."

Laughing, Mason cleared the board, and we spent the remainder of visiting hours playing chess and remembering the good times before murder was a common word in Flamingo Springs.

That night, I struggled to fall asleep even though I was exhausted. My words from earlier circled in my head, and I couldn't get away from the feeling of unease that twisted my stomach. "He's still got one more move." Whoever was still out there wasn't done. No matter what anyone told me, I knew this story wasn't over yet. All I could do was pray that when it was, I'd be around to see it.

"THE WOMAN behind Cody Jackson's near-death rodeo experience, as well as the attempted murder of his fiancée and her two friends, and a suspect in another murder, has finally broken her silence. Rosie O'Conner, twenty-nine, says she'd do anything to help a friend. Even if that includes the alleged murder of that very friend."

I swallowed my bite of bagel, staring at the TV. This wasn't exactly how I'd wanted to start Christmas Eve, and my stomach clenched as the newscaster spoke.

Rosie had been in federal custody for several days now, and Blaze was unable to get much information from the agents in charge of her case. I wondered if he knew she'd talked, or if he was finding out from the morning news like I was.

"I don't regret what I did," the young reporter continued, her dark lipstick making her white teeth gleam as she quoted Rosie. "And given the chance, I'd do it again."

The reporter continued covering the breaking news about Rosie for the next several minutes, and I could only sit frozen on my couch and watch.

Rosie had demanded a deal before agreeing to say much more. When the video switched to an aerial photo of Cody's ranch as the reporter discussed Cody's life with her fellow anchorman, I turned the TV off and sat in silence.

The buzz of my phone startled me, interrupting the dark thoughts that crowded my mind. It was Aubrey.

"They're not saying on the news, but Rosie's plea bargain was to avoid the death penalty," she said. "They agreed, and she's been talking all morning. The FBI videoed Blaze in since the case started here."

"We know why Greg killed Sarah and Dalton. But how is Rosie connected to everything?"

"Rosie is who they were running from," Blaze said, static filling the air for a moment as Aubrey switched me to speakerphone. "Remember, we never could figure out if they were running from someone or if they'd committed a crime and were hiding. Turns out, Rosie was running drugs through one of Sarah's clients at the salon, and Sarah turned them in."

"How did she find them?" I asked quietly, setting my coffee cup on the end table. Grabbing a throw pillow, I hugged it to my chest as Blaze filled me in.

"She was friends with Greg, and I use that term lightly. Greg still dabbled in drugs here and there, and she was his connection. The plan was to wait for her to arrive in town, and they'd take care of Sarah and Dalton together, but after a fight with Dalton over Sarah, Greg lost it and murdered both of them. There's a journal entry in his phone that backs it up."

Squeezing the pillow, I took a deep breath. The coffee I'd just finished threatened to come back up as Aubrey continued talking.

"And that's why she murdered Greg. Rosie said he took

justice away from her, and she killed him for it. But neither were sure if you or Cody knew anything because of how close you were to Dalton and Sarah. That's why she came after you. Mitch and Kasey were innocent bystanders."

"Has she said anything about who helped her?" Voice quiet, I sank back into the corner of the couch, holding my phone so tightly my hand began to cramp.

Blaze sighed, the sound loud in my ear as Aubrey murmured something in the background. "Not yet. But I'm hoping she will."

We hung up a few minutes later, and I stared at the green rug in front of me.

"Oh, Sarah," I whispered. "Why didn't you tell me? We could have helped you. We could have saved you!"

Tears flooded my eyes, but I refused to shed them. I was tired of crying, tired of wondering why. Maybe Audrey was right. Even though we didn't have all the answers and possibly never would, maybe it was time for me to move forward.

Cody was set to be released today, and I debated not going to see him again. I'd found myself unsure about renewing our relationship. He'd changed, as had I, but something held me back from giving him my heart again.

After a few more minutes of deliberation, I got to my feet and slid my sneakers on before grabbing my keys and slipping my phone into my back pocket.

Broken up or not, Cody deserved a good meal to come home to. Both his parents had returned to Oklahoma, and none of his remaining ranch hands knew the first thing about the kitchen. Prepackaged meals and takeout were what Jackson Ranch survived on, but for someone coming home from the hospital, it was the last thing needed.

Locking the door after myself, I made my way down the outside stairs to my car in the back alley. Yesterday's mantra of keeping busy repeated itself in my head, and after stopping at Jesse's Grocery Mart for supplies, I headed out to Cody's ranch.

The dogs greeted me as I pulled into the driveway, and Mason came out of the front barn, wiping his hands on a cloth, his shirt streaked with oil and dirt.

"Where is everyone?" I stepped out of my car and popped the trunk open to grab the groceries. "This place looks deserted!"

"You're not wrong." Mason took a few bags and lead the way to the house. "Four ranch hands have quit in the last week. Counting Tyler and Greg, we've lost six since this all started, and I'm having to outsource from other ranches."

"Why is everyone quitting?" Setting my bags on the kitchen counter, I turned to face Mason, hands on my hips. "Surely not because of what happened with Greg."

Mason carefully placed his bags next to mine before answering, the dogs running past the window, yipping as they played.

"The boys are scared, Lacey. No one knows what's going on, just that two people on this ranch were murdered, and Cody just about bought it too. They don't want to be next, and I don't blame them."

Digging in the cabinet by the stove, I pulled out a frying pan.

"I suppose you're right. But talk about kicking a man when he's down. How is Cody supposed to run the ranch with no help?"

Mason shrugged before leaving the kitchen, talking over his shoulder. "Same way he did when he first started out. Long hours and no breaks. It'll be all right. Always has been, always will be."

Staring after him, I frowned. Cody wouldn't be able to compete for quite some time, and his insurance would only cover so much. If he lost business at the ranch, things could get bad fast.

"Guess I know what's going to be keeping me busy." I slammed the frying pan down on the stove top. I could drive a tractor and herd cattle as good as any ranch hand, and though it was something I thought I'd left in the past, clearly, it wasn't.

"God," I looked up at the kitchen ceiling, "I have no clue what I'm doing. Hopefully, You do."

———

THREE HOURS LATER, a hearty pot of gumbo simmered on the stove, and cornbread baked in the oven. Mason had left not long after our conversation to get Cody from the hospital, and I expected them back any minute.

I trekked to the living room and shifted my gaze out the window across the yard to the bunkhouse. Somehow, it seemed like it'd been only a few days since Aubrey and I had distracted Greg while Jeff rummaged through the ranch hands' belongings looking for clues. At the same time, it felt like it had been months, and my shoulders drooped as I yawned.

With Christmas not even twelve hours away, the ranch was empty, Cody's remaining employees having gone to their respective homes for Christmas as they always did. It put extra work on Cody's shoulders, but he insisted his ranch hands take time to be with their families.

The sound of tires on gravel alerted me to Mason's return the same time the barking of the Luna and Henry did. Leaving the living room, I made my way to the front porch. Mason helped Cody out of the truck, and I crossed my arms over my chest, suddenly cold in the breeze that had sprung up.

"Good to be home," Cody sighed as he slowly climbed the steps to the porch I'd fallen off of not that long ago.

"I'm gonna go finish fixin' that tractor, and I'll be in."

Mason headed toward the barn. "Holler if you need me." Whistling a cheerful song, he crossed the drive, both dogs racing after him.

Cody turned to face me after thanking his new foreman. "Been a wild ride, hasn't it, Lace?" The dark smears of fatigue beneath his eyes matched the navy shirt he wore, the rodeo logo on the upper left corner faded and peeling away from the fabric.

"It's not over yet." I opened the door and ushered him inside. "You're coming back to six fewer ranch hands and a good four months of recovery, and I'm having my entire salon gutted and remodeled before I open again."

"It's all good." He stepped past me and hung his hat up on the rack by the door.

I drew in my breath and then released it before speaking. "How can you say that so cheerfully?" I followed him to the kitchen.

Cody grabbed a glass from the cupboard by the sink and filled it with water from the fridge before turning to face me. Blue eyes serious, he studied me as he took a sip. "It's all good because God's good."

Finding no answer to his calm reply, I brushed past him and gave the pot of gumbo a vicious stir, the smell of spices and seafood filling the air. "Well," I put the lid back on the pot with a clang, "I'll be helping you out much as I can until you're back on your feet and my salon has reopened."

"And I thank you." Cody drained his glass and set it in the sink. He let out a deep sigh. "One day at a time."

Leaving me to finish dinner, he wandered into the living room. When I checked on him minutes later, he was sound asleep, one boot on, the other on its side next to the couch.

Grabbing his jean jacket off the hook by the door, I made my way to the barn and busied myself with the kittens that played in the corner. Mason was still working on the tractor,

Christmas music drifting down from the phone he'd placed on the tractor seat.

"You gonna marry him?" He dug through a toolbox. Sweat and dirt streaked his arms.

I cuddled a kitten to my chest, her yellow fur soft against my chin as I kissed the top of her head. "I don't know," I said after a long pause.

Mason gave me a stern look, finally finding the tool he needed. "It's been what, three, five years? Ain't it about time you two got past that and just took the leap?" Turning, he resumed work on the tractor, the sound of metal on metal making the kitten in my arms jump. Across the barn, Luna and Henry played with a rope toy, their playful growls quiet.

"I think I'll head back to the house," I muttered, setting the kitten back down.

Mason chuckled. "Truth hurts, but you know I'm right."

Stomping out of the barn, I wandered aimlessly across the yard, stopping to watch the chickens mill around before stepping up on the porch. The swing creaked as I sat, wincing a bit as my sore muscles protested.

Giving myself a push, I pulled my feet up, tucking them to the side, and stared across the yard. Jackson territory spread out far in front of me, and for a moment, I let myself pretend Cody and I were married. It'd be about time for him to come in with the kids we'd hoped to have, and I could almost hear him chuckling as he carried them piggyback across the yard.

"None of that," I told myself firmly. "We're taking it one day at a time." Despite my harsh rebuttal, I continued daydreaming about life with the rancher. There'd been a time when we'd had names picked out for our kids, and I sighed as I realized the crossroads I was at.

The sound of my phone chirping in my pocket brought me back to the present and glancing at it, I smiled. Mitch was well enough to work his phone, and the photo he'd sent me showed him grinning as he bit into a burger. Though he was still hooked up to wires and had gauze wrapped around his head, his eyes were clear, and color filled his cheeks.

After I responded to the text, I made my way back into the house where I made a pot of rice. My movements woke Cody, who came and watched me from the doorway, his eyes bleary. A red square on his cheek matched the corner of the cushion he'd fallen asleep on, and I grinned when he yawned.

The sound of the front door banging stopped me from teasing him. Mason trooped down the hallway to the restroom.

"Help me set the table?" I asked, and ten minutes later, we sat down, both men loudly proclaiming their gratitude over the meal.

"I've known you over three years, Lacey," Mason sighed after finishing his second bowl, "and I didn't know you could cook like that."

Shrugging, I took a sip of sweet tea. "It's just gumbo."

Cody snorted. "Mouth-waterin' gumbo." Ladling another helping into his bowl, he gave me a pointed look. "Feel free to cook for us anytime."

Our talk turned to the case, and Mason shook his head as he read the news article I showed him on my phone.

"It's a shame," he said. "Lot of lost lives."

"Flamingo Springs has always been the best place to live." I got to my feet and cleared the table. "But these last six months have been something else."

"You can say that again," Cody mumbled into his glass as he finished his tea.

The conversation shifted to business, and I busied myself with a book while the men crunched numbers. Curled up under a blanket, I drifted off a few pages in and didn't hear Mason leave for the bunkhouse sometime later.

When I woke up, it was close to midnight, and Cody was sound asleep in the recliner next to the couch I'd stretched out on. Christmas music played from the TV channel, which mimicked a fireplace, flames dancing across the screen.

Christmas was in less than ten minutes, and I hadn't wrapped a single gift, baked one cookie, or even written greeting cards. It didn't feel like the holidays, and turning my gaze to Cody, I breathed a prayer of thanks he was still alive.

I debated slipping out and going home, but the only thing that waited for me was a cold bed and an empty fridge. Cody's home was warm and welcoming, and finally, I decided to stay. Snuggling under the blanket, I fell back asleep as another song began to play. Maybe all really was well.

***

"LACEY! LACEY, WAKE UP!"

A strong hand shook my shoulder, the sound of the dogs barking outside interrupting the Christmas music still playing. "Lacey!"

I pried my eyes open. Cody crouched over me. The cough I let out was loud, and my throat stung. Head throbbing, I sat up. The room was filled with smoke.

"We gotta go." Grabbing me by the arms, Cody pulled me to my feet.

Flames already engulfed the kitchen and front entry, and my shirt stuck to my sweat-dampened back as Cody dragged me down the hallway toward the back door.

A loud explosion behind us shook the house. The sound of glass shattering drowned out the dogs now yipping in panic. All traces of sleep disappeared, and my heart pounded against my shirt as we tried to escape the flames.

The back door was located in the middle of the wide hallway, and I shifted my gaze toward the spare bedroom the hall ended at. Flames curled around the bed and inched their way across the wood flooring.

"It's jammed!" Cody wrestled with the handle of the back door, coughing as he did so. The smoke that filled the house was thick and hot, and my eyes burned as I squinted in the wavering red light. "Lacey, I can't get the door open."

Panic filled Cody's voice as he turned to me, his eyes wide as he glanced down the hall. By now, the living room was nothing but a wall of flames, and the sounds of creaking reached our ears above the crackling of the fire.

Pushing me down the hallway, Cody prayed under his breath as we stopped at the entrance of the spare bedroom, more than half of it already consumed. "We're gonna have to go through the window."

"Are you insane?" I faced Cody as he took his sweatshirt off, my feet screaming in pain from the scalding hot floor. "We'll be running straight through the fire!" I had to shout for him to hear me, and my throat burned in protest as I coughed again, my nose stinging.

"We don't have a choice," Cody yelled, wrapping his sweater around my head to protect my hair. "The house is about to come down."

He took a step into the bedroom, and I followed, the heat from the fire so hot it felt like my face was going to melt. The window next to the bed was almost nothing but flames, and fire had completely consumed the wall around the glass panels. The wavering light shone so bright I squinted, and sparks pricked my arms as the flames inched forward.

Grabbing the rocking chair that smoldered, Cody threw it through the window, the tinkling of glass a welcome sound.

The fire surged at the sudden rush of air that filled the room, and the flames from the bed reached out and licked my bare arm. The yelp I let out was hidden beneath the roar behind us in the hallway. Shoving me forward, Cody wrapped his fingers around my belt and tossed me out the window, jumping out after me.

I landed hard and rolled as sparks tried to ignite on my shirt. Cody did the same as flames erupted out of the window and crawled up the side of the house.

"We gotta move," Cody screamed, and getting up, I was only able to take a few steps before falling to my knees, my blistered feet not allowing me to stand.

Pieces of dried weeds and shards of glass bit into my hands and knees as I crawled away from the house on the cold ground, Luna and Henry still barking as they ran back and forth in front of me.

A loud groaning filled the air right before Cody landed on top of me, shielding me with his body as the house collapsed, embers and debris raining down on us. I'd lost the sweater he'd wrapped around my hair when I'd hit the ground, and he covered my neck and head with his forearms.

"Get back!" he yelled at the dogs when they tried to get close, one of them yelping when it stepped on burning debris. Cody yelled another command, and the dogs retreated to a safe distance, both now growling.

Cody pressed my head back down into the dead grass, his weight heavy on me. "Keep your head down and close your eyes."

Hot debris landed on my blistered foot, and I jerked, letting out a pained cry, the taste of dirt and smoke strong in my dry mouth.

The explosion came a moment later, shaking the ground beneath us, and more embers rained down.

Cody's prayers mixed with mine as my dry eyes tried to tear up, both our bodies trembling. The parts of me he wasn't covering stung with little pinpricks of heat as sparks landed on us.

The minutes stretched on, and it was a long time before Cody rolled off me. Getting to our hands and knees, we crawled toward the bunkhouse. The dogs ran to us at Cody's gentle command, Luna licking my face, her whiskers soft against my hot skin while Henry circled Cody, still growling.

Turning, I faced what was left of the house, leaning back on my palms, Cody doing the same. Far enough away to be safe, I could still feel the heat from the red flames, and I glanced at the rancher.

Face somber as he watched the fire, he looped one arm around Henry as Luna sat behind him, resting her chin on his shoulder.

"If they hadn't started barking outside the window, I wouldn't have woken up," he said.

Cold wind blew across the backyard, and I shivered. Luna left Cody to lean against me, her fur warm. "I'm so sorry, Cody."

Cody shrugged, his clothes, like mine, dotted with holes from sparks, his face red in the firelight. "It's just stuff. We both made it out, the dogs are safe, and at the end of it all, that's what matters the most. Stuff can be replaced. We can't."

"I know," I whispered. "I know." We were silent for a moment, and I took several deep breaths, the cold air soothing my burning lungs and scratchy throat.

"There's a landline phone in the bunkhouse. We'll be able to call for help from there and get the first aid kit."

"Think it was on purpose?" I already dreaded the painful walk to the bunkhouse.

"Possibly," Cody said slowly.

"Where's Mason?" Why hadn't he helped us escape the fire?

"Right here."

Cody and I turned around. Mason stood, the pistol he held at his side glinting in the firelight. His shadow was long, the black sky above him filled with smoke and stars.

I'd finally found the last piece of the puzzle. "You're Rosie's accomplice." Luna let out a deep growl at the anger in my voice. The fur on her back rose as I rested my hand on her neck, wrapping my fingers around her thick collar.

"Now that's where you're wrong," Mason said as Cody's mouth slackened as he stared at his new foreman. "It was the other way around."

"I don't understand." I let out a short cough.

"And I don't care to explain." Mason waved the gun at me. "Now, get to your feet. Both of you. The fire was supposed to take care of this once and for all, but you two have more luck than you know what to do with."

"It's not luck." Cody helped me to my feet, both of us wincing in pain. "It's God, and trust me, He's not done."

"Oh, please." The whites of Mason's eyes shone in the firelight as he rolled them. "Don't start with your Jesus talk, Cody. I've heard so much of that the last two months I could quote it in my sleep."

"Good." Cody gave a dry laugh. "Then you can quote it in prison."

"I won't be going to prison any more than you two will be going on a honeymoon," Mason growled. Raising the gun, he pointed it at my midsection. "Make one wrong move, and I'll shoot her."

Cody stiffened, and both dogs growled in earnest, sensing their owner's change in behavior. "Heel." Ater a moment, the dogs quieted.

"The fire would have been so much neater than this." Mason motioned for Cody and me to walk to the bunkhouse. "But at least this way, I'll know for certain you're dead, and I can be on my way." I whimpered in pain, and Mason let out a menacing cackle.

"Forgive me," he said as I limped past him. "It's not that I find pain funny, but I do find yours amusing because you made this whole thing personal when Rosie was arrested."

"Like it's my fault she's a murderer?" I stopped and faced the ranch hand.

Mason stepped toward me as Cody reached out and gave my shoulder a warning squeeze. I shook him off.

"We're gonna die anyway," I told him, shivering as my damp shirt dried in the cool breeze. "So I'm going to say whatever I want to."

Mason cocked his head before waving the gun at me. "You're not wrong." He took another step and shoved me forward. "Now shut up and walk."

Reaching out, I grabbed Cody's hand, the tight squeeze he gave me reassuring. This wasn't how I'd envisioned our future, but if this was the end, I was glad he was with me.

13

Once in the smoke-filled bunkhouse, Mason directed Cody and me to sit on the couch that faced the fireplace. Ranching magazines were strewn across the end table, one crumpled on top of a duffle bag embossed with Mason's name.

"Get comfortable." Mason straddled the kitchen chair in front of the couch. Crossing his arms over the top of its back, he let the gun hang by his side, safety off. I pressed against Cody, and he wrapped his arm around my shoulders.

"Since you're gonna kill us, you could at least tell us why." Cody's voice was dry as he glared at his former friend.

"Nothing personal," Mason assured him, eyes glinting in the light the lamp in the corner offered. "You two are just loose ends that need to be snipped."

"Thing is, we never knew anything." My breath hitched. "You and Rosie could have murdered Sarah, Dalton, and Greg, and no one would have ever known it was you."

"It's not about what you know or don't know." Mason shook his head. "It's the fact that once you two get a taste for something, you don't stop. You would have chased every lead down until eventually, you found the one that would lead to me. That's why Rosie and I decided to silence you."

"You really think you'll get away with this?" Cody asked. "Five murders? And for that matter, Rosie's gonna sell you out. If they offer her another deal, she'll tell them everything they want to know, including your identity."

Mason's jaw clenched as he took a deep breath. "I'm well aware. Which is why as soon as I'm done taking care of you two, I'll be on my way. I've got a flight to catch and some new ID cards to pick up along the way."

"Well, have fun living the rest of your life with this on your conscience." Cody's voice was quiet, and his fingers dug into my shoulder. Outside, Luna and Henry yipped and pawed at the door, knowing something was wrong, and the whinnying of the horses from the barn could be heard above them.

"You think I wanted this?" Mason's tone was incredulous. "I assure you, while Sarah and Dalton needed to pay for what they did to me, I had no intention of killing them. That was completely on Greg and his little jealousy problem from his fling with Sarah in college."

"What they did to you?" Voice hoarse, I stared at the person I would have never suspected of being behind the last few weeks of absolute terror.

"Ratted me and my gang out to the Feds is what they did." Mason reached up and scratched his head with his free hand. The cough he let out was raspy, the smoke beginning to affect him.

"Miami is a hot spot for drugs, and it was easy to run an operation there. Rosie headed everything up since she had so many connections from her college days, but I called all the shots. Sarah's coworker was one of our best sellers, and when Sarah found out, she called the Feds before disappearing with Dalton."

"And Greg? How involved was he really?"

Mason shrugged. "Not a whole lot, actually. He barely knew what was going on, but he liked the cashflow it provided him. If Sarah hadn't caught on to what was happening, my little operation would have spanned states, not just counties, and Tyler would have been my mule for Texas while Greg would have worked Louisiana. You wouldn't believe the connections we were making in the rodeo world thanks to Rosie."

"You're lying," Cody seethed, and I stiffened when Mason waved the gun at him, his finger resting on the trigger.

"Even the best of people will turn for a little money, Cody. Look at what happened to Ryan. Murdered by his own brother, all for some cash."

Mason lowered the gun and looked at me. "Mabel is a perfect example, too, isn't she, Lacey? Murdered Vicki and tried to kill Aubrey, all so she could have her own bakery. It always comes down to money."

"I pay you good money," Cody told his ranch hand, voice so low it was a growl. "If you needed more, all you had to do was ask."

"You got millions to give me, Cody?" Mason asked. "Because that's what these operations bring in. And if Greg hadn't been so eager to act out his little revenge plan, that's what I'd be sitting on right now, and so would Rosie."

"And now she'll never see the outside world again." Tears filled my eyes as I thought of the woman I'd considered a friend and all she'd done to me, Cody, Mitch, and Kasey.

"Again, because she made it personal," Mason told me. "Greg killing Sarah and Dalton threw a wrench in our plans and caused the whole operation to be shut down for good, because we had no idea what they knew or who they'd told and had no way to find out. But killing Greg made it worse."

"And setting fire to the trailer?" Cody loosened his grasp on my arm, his burnt shirt tearing a bit as he shifted, and I winced when his foot brushed mine.

"My idea," Mason admitted. "And I was also the one who carried it out. Drove the six hours to Greshing, started the fire, and got back in town just in time to do a follow-up interview with Blaze. But the whole kidnapping Lacey and her friends? I had nothing to do with that. Rosie became unhinged when she found out we'd lost everything. I'd just sunk every last penny we'd had into expanding our operation, and when the Feds got involved, all my lenders, all the buyers, everyone backed out."

"Oh, what a shame," Cody mocked. "Losing ill-gained funds."

"It was a setback for sure," Mason admitted, ignoring Cody's jab. "But I'd made enough in the last year to not be worried, especially since I still had my paycheck from the ranch. Thing about the illegal drug trade is it'll always be there, and you can always start over because it's in every city. No matter how small, no matter how quaint or tourist friendly, there will always be a demand for it."

"So why not just execute us the way she did Greg?" I said, bringing what could be my last conversation back around to Rosie. "Why rig Cody's gear and put me and my friends through everything she did? She created a bigger mess to clean up, and that's why she got caught."

"Like I said," Mason answered, standing and leaning to one side to stretch his back. "Losing all the money made it personal for her and she wanted you to suffer." He gave me a pointed look. "And besides, rigging Cody's gear was a lot easier than sneaking up on him."

Yawning, he fixed his gaze on me. "It wasn't easy to convince Tyler to cut that fence and stampede those cattle on you. Even after I assured him it was just a scare tactic and nothing more, he hesitated, but in the end, the thought of his old gang being told where he was proved to be the right amount of pressure to get him to do whatever I wanted." Shoving the chair across the floor with his foot, he brought the gun up again and pointed it at my chest.

"Now, I've satisfied your curiosity and have just enough time to get my ID cards and make my flight." He squinted as his finger tightened on the trigger. "It's nothing personal, you understand. Except, at this point, it kinda is."

Cody pulled me tight against him, his heart thudding against his ribs. Wrapping my arms around his waist, I stared at Mason.

"I lost the only woman I've ever loved when they arrested Rosie," Mason said. "And I want you to know how that feels, Cody." Eyes switching to me, his mouth twitched. "Ladies first."

The gunshot was loud in the large room, but so was Mason's scream when Luna latched onto his arm, pulling it down, the front door having not fully latched, letting the herding dog in. The bullet went through the couch right between my calves and exited the back of it, continuing its destructive path into the kitchen where it hit something metal.

Luna's growls filled the air, the dog swinging in the air as Henry charged in, going after Mason's leg.

Cody was almost to the squabble when Mason grabbed the gun he'd dropped, the discharge making my ears ring as he shot Luna. Her scream turned to a muted yelp as she dropped to the floor, the blood from the wound in her shoulder mixing with Mason's as it dripped from her teeth, her lip still curled.

Henry snarled as he shook his head, tearing the fabric of Mason's pants away from his leg. Before Mason could aim at the dog, Cody landed on him, both men falling to the hard floor, the gun skittering into the fireplace.

Still weak from his time in the hospital and escaping the house fire, Cody was quickly overwhelmed by Mason, who slammed his head against the floor. The kick the ranch hand aimed at Henry landed hard, and the dog slid across the floor, yipping. Luna let out a weak bark, trying to stand, her shoulder gushing blood onto the wood floor.

"God, give me strength," I whispered, leaving the couch and jumping over the two men, trying to get to the fireplace.

Mason grabbed my ankle as I went past him, and I landed hard on the stone edge, feeling something crack in my chest.

"Let her go!" Cody's roar was almost louder than the gunshot had been. I glanced over my shoulder. He struggled against Mason, and blood dripped from his nose.

Reaching out, I grasped the butt of the pistol, my wrist screaming in pain as it pressed against the coals hidden beneath the ash in the fireplace. Teeth gritted as Mason released his hold on my foot to fully turn on Cody, I grabbed the gun and rolled over, pointing it at the two.

"Drop it or he's dead!" The hunting knife Mason held to Cody's throat glinted, and a drop of blood appeared he pressed it against Cody's skin.

"I drop it, and he's still dead," I argued, heart pounding as I stared into Cody's bloodshot blue eyes.

By now, Henry's yips had subsided, and Luna was still, a pool of blood now surrounding her and spreading to the rug.

"Shoot him," Cody said, voice firm. "This has to end."

Finger tightening on the trigger, I shifted my gaze to look directly into Mason's eyes as I pointed the gun at his head. Free hand coming up to cup the bottom of the gun, I swallowed hard. "Drop the knife, Mason. It's over."

"And go to prison for the rest of my life? No, I'll die first." Mason's voice was panicked as he pressed the knife against Cody's neck. Cody winced, a steady trickle of blood dripping from the edge of the blade.

"You haven't killed anyone, Mason," I told the wild-eyed drug dealer. "You don't want that on your mind for the rest of your life. And no matter how far you run, they'll find you."

Neck aching from holding my head up, I worked to keep my voice even as the ledge of the fireplace dug into my back.

"Lacey, shoot him!" Cody's voice was weaker than before, and I glanced at him, wishing he'd be quiet. When I'd grabbed the gun, I'd accidentally released the magazine and therefore was pointing a useless weapon at Mason. I could only hope he didn't look past me and see the magazine laying in the ashes. "There's still time to turn around," I told Mason. "And deep down, you know you don't want to kill anyone."

The air was heavy as Mason stared into my eyes. Flames crackled outside as the fire from the house spread across the dry yard, and my nose burned from its acrid smell.

God, I trust You. Just like You were in the fiery furnace with the three Hebrew boys, I know You're with Cody and me right now. The simple prayer caused the shaking in my arms to cease, and after a long pause, I lowered the gun.

"Lacey!" Cody's weak cry was enraged as he stared at me in disbelief.

"I won't." Taking a deep breath, I brought the gun all the way down so it rested on my thigh. "Mason, it's not that I can't, but I won't. I've seen too much death in the last six months to believe that adding to it is the answer."

A large drop of sweat trickled down Mason's nose as his reddened eyes widened. Henry's nails clicked on the floor as the injured dog limped toward Luna, dragging his back leg. Mason flinched at the sound, the bead of sweat falling on Cody's shoulder.

"Put the knife down, Mason," I said softly. "It's over. We can get you help."

The seconds ticked by as Mason considered my words, his face losing its redness.

His grip loosened on Cody's neck, and it was all Cody needed to jerk away and gain the upper hand. Years of hogtying and roping cattle came in handy, and a few minutes later, Mason was completely bound, his head resting in Luna's blood.

"We gotta get that fire out," Cody told me, hand pressed to the cut on his throat, blood seeping between his fingers. "With the grass as dry as it is, we could have a wildfire on our hands if we don't."

The next thirty minutes raced by as we worked to put the fire out, the water from the hose attached to the barn cold against our burnt hands. Cody's house was gone, but the air was still hot from the flames that had crept almost all the way across the yard to the bunkhouse. The chickens clucked nervously in their coop as I dumped bucket after bucket on the corner that smoked, Cody working to finish putting out the flames in the south part of the yard.

Blaze and Jeff were on their way, answering my call from the landline in the bunkhouse on the first ring. Jeff gave me first aid instructions over the phone to care for Luna once I was able to leave Cody to put out the final few flames. The herding dog's pulse was almost non-existent, and I doubted she'd make it much longer.

Henry rested his head on my knee as I tended to Luna, his whimpers low as he stared at her. The drool that foamed around his mouth was pink with blood, and he occasionally let out a weak whimper, his hind leg clearly broken.

Mason glared at me from across the room where he lay tied up on the floor, Cody having moved him so he was against the wall. The threats he'd screamed at me had caused me to stuff a rag in his mouth, and I ignored his muffled words as I stroked Henry's head.

The front door swung open, letting in a cool breeze, and I sent up a prayer of thanks that the latch was loose, as it was what had let the dogs in. Looking back down at Luna, I traced my thumb over her ear, wiping away the tears that had dripped from my chin.

The rest of the night was a blur once Jeff and Blaze arrived. Sliding across the gravel, both were out of the cruiser almost before Blaze had it in park. The bright headlights made me squint as they shone through the front window of the bunkhouse.

Jeff did what he could for the dogs before loading them into his truck and heading to his clinic, but he was hopeful both would pull through. Luna's wound looked far worse than it was, and the herding dog had weakly licked my hand before Jeff shut the truck door.

Blaze handcuffed the ranch hand, his green eyes heavy with fatigue. Once Mason was locked in the back of his cruiser, Blaze made calls, boot heels loud on the floor as he paced the kitchen, resting his free hand on the butt of his gun.

Terri and Aubrey showed up not long after he left, and they rendered first aid to Cody and me. Once our feet were bandaged and Cody's neck was seen to, they gave us a moment alone, the rest of our injuries minor enough to be taken care of later.

Pink and gold beams of early morning sunlight streaked across the sky over the south pasture, and the air lost its chilliness. Smoke still hung above us, but a calmness surrounded me even as we walked through the ashes of what had been Cody's home.

It wasn't how I thought I'd be spending Christmas morning, but after everything I'd been through, I wouldn't have wanted it any other way.

The cowboy hat Cody had dug from the backseat of his truck sat snug on his head as he wrapped an arm around my waist. I chuckled as we limped away from what was left of his house.

"Still can't believe there were no bullets," Cody said, sounding equally amused and horrified as the chickens exited their coop and poked their way around our feet.

"And I still can't believe we walked out of that alive." I leaned against him.

We fell silent, watching the sun rise. Out of the corner of my eye, I saw Cody turn to look at me, and I knew if I faced him, he'd kiss me.

The gentle squeeze he gave my waist was all the encouragement I needed, and carefully turning on painful feet, I met his blue eyes. The rest of the world faded away as he stared back, his gaze softening as he studied me. I'd expected butterflies to take over my stomach, but instead, I was overwhelmed by peace.

Twitching his lips, Cody reached up and took his hat off. He plunked it on my head before pulling me against him, slipping one hand up to tangle in my hair. Lowering his lips to mine, he tasted like smoke and a thousand promises.

I cupped his face, pressing against his chest as he tightened his arms around me, his hands warm on my back and neck.

The stubble on his chin felt rough against my skin as he pulled away and leveled me with a long look.

"What?" I stared at him.

Cody quirked an eyebrow, a grin teasing the corner of his mouth as he took in the effect he had on me. "Know what it means when a cowboy puts his hat on a woman and kisses her?"

My cheeks flushed as he rested his hands on the small of my back. "I don't. Do tell."

"It means she's his woman," Cody drawled, bending so his lips brushed mine as he spoke. Eyes twinkling, he gave me a toothy grin. "You all right with that?"

"I—I most certainly am," I stammered, the brim of the hat brushing against his forehead.

"Perfect," he whispered, and bending me back, he kissed me with such passion, I found myself clinging to him as my legs buckled. Hands tangled in the tattered remains of his shirt, I kissed him back with every bit of love I'd been suppressing for the last several months, and I felt him smile against my lips.

"Merry Christmas, Lacey," he said a long moment later, cheeks flushed. Going down on one knee, he looked up at me as he grasped my trembling hands. "Now, the third time didn't quite work like a charm for us, but I think the fourth will."

"I know so," I whispered, tears sliding down my cheeks.

"I don't have a ring, but Lacey Baker, will you marry me?"

"Yes," I sobbed, leaning forward and flinging my arms around him. "I can't think of anything I'd love to do more!"

Standing, Cody held me tight, his heart pounding against my ear as I buried my face in his chest. The noise of the ranch faded away as we turned and watched the sun crest the horizon, golden light flooding the pastures.

Just as a new day was beginning, so was our future, and I couldn't wait to see what God had in store for us.

With God by our side, there was nothing we couldn't face. His love for us is always and forever, and knowing that was all I would ever need.

The End

ACKNOWLEDGMENTS

Diane Burns, your insight on the bits and pieces of rough draft I'd send you in the middle of the night are what brought this book together, and this trilogy wouldn't be possible without you.

ABOUT THE AUTHOR

Keri Lynn discovered her love for writing before she'd even completed kindergarten, and that passion has only grown over the years. She has had several poems published and plans to continue expanding her genres. When the Wisconsin born writer isn't busy creating new worlds, she can be found experimenting in the kitchen, writing music, exploring waterfalls, and spending time with her family. She resides in Summertown, Tenn.

ALSO BY KERI LYNN

Pancakes, Bacon, and a Side of Murder

by Keri Lynn

A Texas-Sized Mystery - Book One

Flamingo Springs, Texas. Owning a bakery has always been Aubrey Turner's dream. Finding her rival's dead body was not part of it. When new sheriff Blaze Martin puts her at the top of his suspect list, she's left with no choice but to try to solve the mystery herself with the help of two friends. With the Fourth of July bash only days away, the town is overtaken by tourists and YouTube celebrities, and it becomes difficult to discern between friend and foe. But when the killer returns and makes an attempt on Aubrey's life, she realizes that time is running out and she must discover who is behind the attacks before she joins her dead competition.

Get your copy here:

https://scrivenings.link/pancakesbaconandasideofmurder

Not a Good Day for Namaste

by Keri Lynn

A Texas-Sized Mystery - Book Two

Witnessing the hit and run of fellow Flamingo Springs resident Ryan wasn't how yoga instructor Misty Van Oepen planned on starting the Thanksgiving holidays.

When Ryan's mysterious brother shows up along with a spree of crime, she decides it's up to her and fellow business owners Lacey and Jeni, to find out what's going on. After an attempt on Misty's life lands her in protective custody at deputy Stetson Owens' ranch, she finds herself in danger of losing her heart to the former bull rider.

With time running out, will Misty succeed in discovering who's behind the attacks? Or will she fail and become the next victim?

Get your copy here: https://scrivenings.link/notagooddayfornamaste

MORE MYSTERIES FROM SCRIVENINGS PRESS

Show Me Betrayal by Ellen E. Withers

Show Me Mysteries—Book One

Two deaths occur decades apart. Is it possible these deaths are related? What motivates a killer, who got away with murder sixty years ago, to kill again? Was it uncontrollable rage or the hope of silencing someone who fit all the puzzle pieces together and deduced who committed the crime?

Set in the picturesque town of Mexico, Missouri, *Show Me Betrayal* takes flight in words and emotions of rich characters woven together into a story you won't want to put down.

Get your copy here:

https://scrivenings.link/showmebetrayal

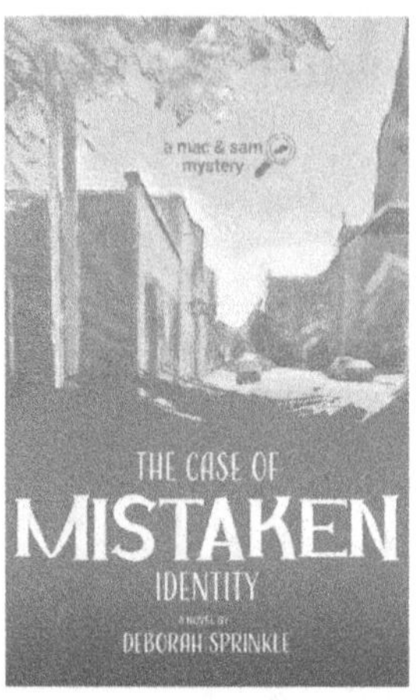

The Case of Misaken Identity by Deborah Sprinkle

A Mac & Sam Mystery—Book Two

Private Investigator Mackenzie Love manages to get into trouble on a simple shopping trip where she finds herself at the business end of a gun. It's clear her attacker mistakes her for someone else, but who? And why is her look-alike in so much trouble?

Mac enlists the help of her partners, Samantha Majors and Miss P, and Detective Jake Sanders to find her doppelgänger and solve the case of mistaken identity.

In the meantime, Mr. Fischer of Fischer Industries comes to the private detectives for help with a problem of his own. As Mac and Sam work on his case, they begin to wonder if the two cases are related.

Can Mac and Sam unravel the clues and get justice for both Mac's look-alike and Mr. Fischer?

Get your copy here:

https://scrivenings.link/mistakenidentity

***True Blue Christmas* by Susan Page Davis**

True Blue Mysteries—Book Five

New neighbors, cryptic Christmas cards, and jury duty. What next? Campbell McBride is juggling her new role as a private investigator with her slightly wacky personal life. Can she and her dad figure out who stashed a valuable painting in their client's attic? And is the murder of an egocentric landlord somehow connected?

Coming November 7, 2023:

https://scrivenings.link/truebluechristmas

Stay up-to-date on your favorite books and authors with our free e-newsletters.

ScriveningsPress.com